JENNEY CHEEVER

A Creature of Habit

Honey Bee
PRESS

Library of Congress Control Number 2025924522

First edition

ISBN: 979-8-9937011-0-3

This book was professionally typeset on Reedsy.
Find out more at reedsy.com

For my Favorites:
Annabelle, Theo, Lorelei and Eric

And for Thomas,
who knew I was a writer, long before I did.

Contents

Acknowledgments

Many thanks to my patient and kind husband, Eric, for being such a good sport about all of the insane ideas I've come up with over the years, for offering support and encouragement, and for reading several versions of this book while it was a mess in progress. And also, for coffee.

Thank you to my children, who inspire me everyday to want to be a better person than I was the day before. They are the lights of my life, and my reason for everything.

Thanks, also, to my sister, Angie, who did a magic trick of transforming from the little sister I used to take care of, into the competent, accomplished woman who supports and guides me in so many ways. Without her knowledge and expertise, this book would have died on my desktop.

And, thank you to Professor Dave Champoux, for assigning the short story that birthed Leonard, and for the invaluable guidance in growing that story into this book.

And finally, thank you so very much to the the friends and family who have taken the time to read the various stories and nonsense I've written over the years, and have encouraged me to keep writing.

Acknowledgments

Prologue

Tuesday, September 18, 2018

Leonard's heartbeat thumped like a drum in his ears, and his head swam. The pavement felt cold and rough under his cheek, and he was aware of a burning, stinging sensation in his palms and knees. He noticed sounds around him, far away and muffled, as if he was underwater. Did someone just say his name?

He sat up, and fought to open his eyes against the glare of the sun. His glasses were dangling from one ear, the lenses resting between his nose and upper lip. He pushed them up to their proper location, and tried to focus. A woman's face was peering down at him, the morning sun surrounding her head like a halo. Leonard wondered if maybe he had actually died.

"ARE YOU OK??" The Angel asked him. "Should I call 911?"

Chapter 1

2018

Leonard J. Thompson has lived in the same New England town his whole life. For the first twenty-six years, he lived with his mother and father, in a small, ranch-style house on a quiet, tree-lined street. For the past thirty-four years, Leonard has lived on his own, in a tidy townhouse condominium, near the center of town, about a half mile from the house he grew up in.

If you were to pass by Leonard J. Thompson on the street, it is unlikely he would draw your attention. He is relatively fit for a sixty-year-old man, due to his habit of walking everyday, but aside from that, he is fairly average in appearance. He is five feet, ten inches tall, and weighs about one hundred and sixty pounds. His graying hair is trimmed once a month at the local barber shop, in the same standard-issue, short hairstyle he's worn since he was a boy. He is always clean-shaven, and wears the type of wire-rimmed glasses that are never really in style or out of style. Generally speaking, Leonard has a tendency to blend into his surroundings, and he prefers it that way. He is definitely not the sort of person who likes to draw attention to himself.

Leonard is what some people might call a "creature of habit." Every morning, he wakes up at precisely 6:30am. After he showers and shaves, he gets dressed in a pair of chinos and a crisply-ironed cotton shirt, then he retrieves the daily newspaper from the front stoop. At 6:55am every day, he sits at his kitchen table and does the daily crossword puzzle, while he eats his Maple and Brown Sugar Quaker Instant Oatmeal. His dear mother, God rest her soul, always said, "A tidy home is a happy home," so he always makes sure his breakfast dishes are washed, dried and put away before he heads out to catch the 8:07 bus to his job at Meyer & Son Manufacturing. Leonard always punches in at exactly 8:30am on the nose. He is quite proud of the fact that, in all of the thirty-seven years he's been at Meyer & Son, he has never been late to work, not even once.

Leonard is in charge of payroll at Meyer & Son. He had originally been hired for an entry level position in the bookkeeping department, soon after he graduated from college, but he eventually worked his way up to his current position as Payroll Manager. At Meyer & Son, Leonard is known for his meticulous work habits. He is the sort of fellow who believes that one should always put forth one's best effort. As his dear mother, God rest her soul, used to say, "Anything worth doing is worth doing well." Some of his fellow employees have been known to tease him a bit, about his diligence and strict attention to detail, but Leonard understands all too well the importance of accuracy in his line of work. Just one small, careless mistake, like transposed numbers or a misplaced decimal point, can really ruin a person's day.

Leonard enjoys the predictable routine of his workday. After he punches in each morning, he heads down the hall to his office, where he spends his mornings at his desk, managing the payroll software, generating payroll reports and making sure the company paychecks are processed accurately and on time. At 12:00pm, Leonard takes his lunch break. He eats his Cup O'Noodles in the employee break room, then visits the lavatory before heading back to his office.

Every afternoon, Leonard has office hours, to meet with employees who need to update their records, or reconcile discrepancies. Lately, however, he has noticed that most of this sort of business in done through the new online portal, or by email. In fact, all of the younger employees seem to prefer these types of communication to meeting face to face. When he was first in charge of payroll, he had, at the very least, met each of his fellow employees, even if he didn't know them well. Now, by Leonard's estimation, there are at least four or five employees on the payroll who he has never even seen in person. While Leonard is certainly one who appreciates efficiency, he does feel that this new way of doing things has made the workplace a lot less personal.

Leonard always wraps up his work for the day by 4:55pm. Then, he straightens up his desk, packs up his briefcase, and punches out at 5:00pm on the nose.

4

Chapter 2

November 1941

The first time that Florence Anderson saw Earl Thompson, she was sitting at her desk at Randall and Bernstein Accounting and Tax Preparation Services, where she'd been employed as a receptionist for the past three years. When she'd seen his name on Mr. Randall's appointment calendar— Earl was scheduled to interview for the Accountant position— she'd imagined he would be middle-aged, hunched, and bespectacled, like the others who had interviewed for the position. So she was quite surprised to see such a tall, slim, handsome fellow walk through the door. He looked to be around her age, mid-twenties, and was absolutely the most attractive man she'd ever seen. He'd tripped a little on the threshold as he came through the door. Florence pretended not to notice, to spare him embarrassment, instead focusing her attention on tidying her already-tidy desk. If anything, his stumble had made him all the more appealing. Florence did her best to look professional, in spite of the butterflies in her stomach. His face was a bit flushed as he approached her desk.

"Good Morning! How may I help you?" Said Florence.

"Hello... My name is Earl Thompson... I have an appointment at nine, for an interview?"

"Oh, yes... Mr. Randall is expecting you, Mr. Thompson."

His blue eyes were lovely. Florence tried not to stare. Instead, she stood up, and gestured for Earl to follow her.

"Right this way, please."

Earl thanked her, and they walked down a hallway, toward the open door of Mr. Randall's office, where the stern, gray-haired Certified Public Accountant was sitting behind a huge desk, piled high with papers.

"Mr. Thompson is here, Mr. Randall." Florence announced.

As she turned to head back down the hall to her desk, she smiled at Earl again.

Florence hoped that Earl Thompson would be hired, so she'd have the chance to get to know him. She was a little disappointed when Mr. Randall asked her to send a letter to Earl, informing him that they would not be requiring his services. As Florence typed up the letter for Mr. Randall, she assumed she'd never see Mr. Thompson again.

But it turns out that Florence wasn't the only one who was smitten that day. Earl's heart had skipped a beat when Florence smiled at him. He'd noticed that she had an adorable dimple in her right cheek, and he was quite taken with the spray of freckles across her nose and cheeks, which were the exact same shade of brown as her sensibly-cut, curly hair. He also noticed that her eyes were the same shade of dark, olive green as the cardigan sweater she had draped over her shoulders.

The weeks leading up to his interview at Randall and Bernstein had been difficult for Earl. He'd been declared "unfit to serve" by the United States Army, due to his asthma, and he was

6

exhausted from weeks of perusing the Help Wanted section of the newspaper and pounding the pavement in search of employment. But after he met Florence Anderson, the world seemed a little brighter. He couldn't stop thinking about her.

One evening, a few weeks after his interview, Earl was just outside the dry cleaners, which was next to the door leading to Randall and Bernstein's office. He saw Florence coming out the door as she was leaving work for the day, and invited her to join him for coffee. It would be many years before Earl would confess to her that their meeting that evening was not a coincidence. He'd gone there deliberately, hoping he might see her.

They began spending time together regularly, often meeting for dinner after work, or going out to see a movie together on the weekends. When they'd first started dating, there had been a few whispers around town, about what that handsome, tall drink of water was doing with plain ol' Florence Anderson. It's true that they were opposites in many ways; Earl was tall and slim, with golden blond hair and pale blue eyes. Florence was short and full-figured, with curly brown hair, and dark, hazel-green eyes. Earl was always dressed impeccably, usually in a pressed suit and polished wingtips, not unlike the leading men in Hollywood movies. Florence, on the other hand, dressed for practicality and comfort, favoring simple cotton dresses, hand-knit sweaters, and sensible shoes. Earl was soft spoken and reserved, while Florence was more outgoing and friendly.

The young couple were oblivious to the gossip, though even if they had heard it, they wouldn't have cared. When they'd first met, at her office, Florence was utterly charmed by Earl's shy, slightly awkward demeanor, which seemed at odds with his movie-star good looks. But as she got to know him, she found his kindness, his intelligence, and his dry sense of humor to be simply irresistible. And Earl felt like the luckiest man alive, to have found a girl like Florence. From the moment he first saw her, he'd been taken by her adorable freckles, that cute little dimple in her cheek, and the way her eyes crinkled at the corners when she laughed, which she did easily and often. But when she had suggested that they go to the library for their second date, he knew he was in love.

Chapter 3

July 31, 2018

As usual, Leonard wrapped up his work for the day by 4:55pm, then straightened up his desk and packed up his briefcase. He punched out at 5pm on the nose, and headed out to catch his bus back home. By 5:25, as usual, he walked up his front steps and checked his mailbox. As often happens, he saw his next door neighbor, Patty, on her way out to walk her dog, Barney.

"Hi, Leonard! Nice evening, isn't it?" Said Patty.

"It certainly is." Replied Leonard.

He tucked the stack of mail under his arm, and unlocked his front door.

Patty is a nurse at the hospital, and is often dressed in colorful scrubs and white clogs. Some of the scrubs she wears are the kind with whimsical prints, such as smiling puppies, or bright sunflowers, or frogs riding tricycles. Patty moved into the townhouse right next to Leonard's with her dog, Barney, five years ago, after divorcing her good-for-nothing husband, Todd. Leonard likes living next door to Patty. He finds her to be a much more pleasant neighbor than his last one, a cranky elderly woman by the name of Mrs. Lebowitz.

While Patty is a friendly neighbor, and always says "hello" to Leonard, Mrs. Lebowitz's favorite pastime seemed to have been shouting at anyone who came within thirty feet of their duplex. He lived next door to her for well over a year before she stopped accusing him of trespassing. Also, she had the annoying habit of keeping her television turned up to maximum volume, because she hated to wear her hearing aids. Leonard could hear every word of her television programs blaring through the shared wall between their living rooms. The good news was, when she was busy watching television, she wasn't shouting out the window. Leonard tried to be compassionate; he figured that she must have had a difficult life, to be so bitter and angry. He did his best to force a smile and say nice things to her, but that only seemed to make her even angrier. Leonard hated to admit it, but he was a bit relieved the day that Mrs Lebowitz's daughter arrived with a U-haul, to take her mother to live with her and her family in Albany. Having had the experience of living next door to Mrs. Lebowitz for so many years makes Leonard all the more appreciative to have someone like Patty for a neighbor.

The first thing Leonard does when he comes in from work each day is sort through the day's mail. He has a very efficient system for this. He immediately puts the junk mail into the recycling bin next to his desk, then puts the bills that need to be paid in a folder marked "bills." Any other items which require his attention go into the paper tray on his desk. Once the mail was sorted, he headed into the kitchen.

Every evening, at exactly 5:45pm, Leonard has some Camp-bell's soup for dinner while reads the newspaper at his kitchen table. Then, after his dinner dishes are washed, dried, and put away, he likes to relax in the living room with a good book. He always goes to bed at 9pm on the dot. His dear mother, God rest her soul, always said, "Early to bed, early to rise, makes a man healthy, wealthy and wise." Imagine Leonard's surprise, when he learned in school that it was actually Ben Franklin who'd said it first.

Chapter 4

August 2013

As Patty ended the call with her Realtor, she checked the time on her iPhone. She still had twenty minutes left on her break...just enough time to grab a quick bite. She walked briskly toward the hospital cafeteria, feeling some of the tension she'd been holding in her neck and shoulders finally beginning to ease up. The last year had been unbearable, but for the first time in several months, she felt a bit of hope. She'd just had her offer accepted on a two-bedroom townhouse condo, in a nice little duplex, right in the center of town. It's less than fifteen minutes away from the hospital, so getting to and from work will be a breeze. The kitchen is a little bit on the small side, but the bathroom was recently renovated, the HOA fees are reasonable, and, according to the Realtor, it's a nice, dog-friendly neighborhood. There's even a dog park nearby. Patty smiled, thinking about how much Barney is going to love that.

"Hey, Patty!" Patty was so lost in her own thoughts, she hadn't noticed that Karen was ahead of her in the line for the cash register. "I haven't seen you smile like that in forever!"

"Oh, Karen! Sorry... " she said, a little embarrassed. "I just got some good news.... Finally."

"Oh, good! Come sit with me." Said Karen, swiping her debit card.

When Patty first started working in the Emergency Department nine years ago, it was a very big change from the post-op floor she'd been working on before. On the post-op floor, you had a pretty good idea of what you'd be dealing with each day. Except for the occasional unexpected complication, it was fairly consistent. But the ED was a whole different kind of nursing. Anything could happen, and it usually did. Especially if you were working the overnight shift. She was so overwhelmed at first, unaccustomed to the extra adrenaline coursing through her body during every shift. But Karen had taken Patty under her wing, and had shown her the ropes. Over the years, they'd become good friends as well as colleagues.

Patty carried her tray over to Karen's table. "So...my offer was accepted on the condo!"

"I knew it! Sit, and tell me!" Karen grinned, pointing to the chair across from her.

"My Realtor thinks we should be able to close by early October." she said, sitting down. "I'm so relieved. I cannot wait to get out of the house. Every corner reminds me of Todd, that good-for-nothing leech."

"Amen to that!" Said Karen, popping a crouton into her mouth.

Patty smiled. "Pretty soon I'll have a home that's all my own. And, I can decorate it however I want. The first thing I am going to buy myself is a brand new bed, and the prettiest floral sheets I can find."

"Good for you!" Karen said. "You deserve it."

"Do you know that for twenty years I have not had floral

sheets? Because Todd insisted that 'Real men don't sleep on flowers.' Where does he get this stuff?"

Karen rolled her eyes. "That man is a piece of work."

"I know! I mean, I'm pretty sure that 'real men' can hold a job for more than six months, and 'real men' don't have sex with Walmart cashiers while their wives are out working, but Todd was certainly not too worried about those things."

"Honest to God, Patty, I don't know how the hell you put up with his bullshit for as long as you did. If he were my husband, I'd already be serving a prison sentence for driving my truck into his sorry ass."

Patty laughed. "I believe you would have. Anyway, I'm counting the days until he's no longer my problem. Ugh. I can't believe I gave that loser the best years of my life."

"Hogwash." Said Karen. Your best years are still to come."

"I'm about to turn fifty!" Patty exclaimed."

"Exactly. I speak from experience. Turning fifty is liberating. And also... fifty is the new thirty! You're still hot."

"Lukewarm, maybe." Patty laughed. You should have seen my ass when I first married Todd. It was amazing."

"A cute little butt will only get you so far. I'll tell you what... I'd take the experience and wisdom of my fifties over my firm but naive thirty year old ass any day of the week." Karen said. "There is tremendous joy in watching your last fuck fly away with the last of your estrogen. It's amazing. You'll see."

"You make a convincing argument." Patty checked the time on her phone. "Ooh, I need to get back." She stood, picking up her tray. "But hey... thanks for the encouragement, Karen. I appreciate it."

"Anytime." Karen replied. "I'm really glad you're finally finding your way out of this. You deserve to be happy. You're my favorite co-worker. Don't tell the others."

Patty smiled, and made a zipper motion across her lips.

Chapter 5

November 1942

Ever since Earl Thompson had first begun courting Florence Anderson, her parents had been hoping he would propose. Their daughter was already twenty-six years old, and, as they often reminded her, she wasn't getting any younger. Florence's sister, Eleanor, was twenty-four years old, and had been married for almost five years already.

It hadn't been much of a surprise that Eleanor had married first. She was known as "the pretty one" while Florence was "the smart one," and everyone knew that "smart" was not likely to land a girl a husband. Mrs Anderson had been quite distressed when Florence had entered her twenties with no suitors in sight. To improve Florence's marital prospects, Mrs Anderson suggested to her daughter that she should maybe put on a little lipstick once in a while, for God's sake.

Mrs Anderson was very much relieved that, even without the help of lipstick, Earl and Florence had managed to find each other, and had fallen deeply in love. And so, when Earl bought a ring for Florence, and visited the Anderson home to ask Dr and Mrs Anderson for their blessing, they gave it, quite enthusiastically. Then, on a crisp, autumn afternoon, one year after his fateful interview at Randall & Bernstein, Earl got down on one knee, in front of the steps to the library, and held up a small box.

"Florence Anderson, will you marry me?"

Florence immediately burst into happy tears, which made it difficult to speak, but she did manage to nod her acceptance, much to Earl's delight.

As Earl slipped the ring onto Florence's finger, the elderly couple who'd just come out of the library, and the group of teen girls walking past on their way to the soda fountain, all stopped and applauded for the happy couple.

As was common practice at the time, it was decided by Mr. Randall and Mr. Bernstein that Florence would no longer work as their receptionist after her wedding, because she'd have a husband to look after. Many years later, with the benefit of hindsight and life experience, Florence will look back on this and find it absolutely absurd. But at the time, it never occurred to her to question it, because it was simply the way things were done back then. Florence, herself, had been hired when their previous receptionist had gotten married. So, she trained the girl who would replace her, then she focused her attention on the business of becoming Mrs Earl Thompson.

That summer, on a cloudy Saturday afternoon, Earl Thompson and Florence Anderson were married at St. Luke's Episcopal church. It was a lovely wedding. Florence's gown, which she sewed herself, was ivory satin, with a delicate floral lace overlay. Her bridal bouquet, cut from her mother's garden, was a cheerful bunch of colorful summer blooms: daisies, roses, lilies, yarrow and lavender, tied together with a satin ribbon. Florence's sister, Eleanor, was the matron of honor, and Earl's best friend from college was the best man. Eleanor's children were the ring bearer and flower girl. They were adorable, of course... especially when little Nancy, who was just barely two, stopped halfway down the aisle to look around and wave at all the people smiling at her.

After the ceremony, and before the reception, they had photos taken. After all the group photos of the bridal party, and the bride and groom with their families, it was time for the close-up portraits of the bride and groom. Since Florence was only five feet, two inches tall, and Earl was six feet, one inch, the photographer had Florence stand on a box, to make it easier to fit them both in the frame. Florence's mother, who had very strong opinions about things being done in a proper and dignified manner, was simply undone at the idea of her daughter, the bride, being asked to stand on an old peach crate, of all things. Both Florence and Earl found the whole situation to be hilarious. If you looked closely at that photo, which hung in the hallway of their home throughout their marriage, you'd see their eyes moist with tears and their faces slightly flushed from laughing.

For the rest of their life together, Florence loved to hear her beloved Earl tell people the story of how they met at Randall & Bernstein's office... how he lost out on the job, but then got the girl, which was even better.

Chapter 6

Saturday, August 4, 2018

Leonard woke up at 6:30am, as he always does on Saturday mornings. After he showered, shaved, and got dressed in an older pair of chinos and a worn-in cotton shirt, he retrieved the daily newspaper from the front stoop. Then, he sat down at the kitchen table to do the crossword puzzle, while he ate his Maple and Brown Sugar Quaker Instant Oatmeal. His dear mother, God rest her soul, always said, "A tidy home is a happy home," so he made sure his breakfast dishes were washed, dried and put away, then got started on his regular weekly household chores. He dusted and vacuumed, cleaned the bathroom, changed the sheets, did his laundry and ironed all of his shirts for the week.

After he had his peanut butter and jelly sandwich for lunch, he headed out, list in hand, to run his weekly errands. Because it was the first Saturday of the month, his first stop was the barber shop, to get his monthly haircut. Next stop was the library, to pick up some new books for the week. This happens to be Leonard's favorite errand.

While on his way to the library, he thought about how, when was a growing up, he had gone there at least once a week with his dear mother, God rest her soul. He remembers that when he was about four years old, he noticed another child, a bit older than himself, checking out her own books, with her own library card. He asked his mother if he could get his own library card, too. She told him that as soon as he was old enough to write his name on the back of a card, he would, indeed, be able to have one of his very own, and would be permitted to check out his own books. The idea of this thrilled Leonard, so he practiced for weeks, writing *Leonard J. Thompson* over and over, on little scraps of paper. Back in those days, the Head Librarian was Mrs. Lewis, who wore her hair piled atop her head in a great silvery mound, lacquered with so much hairspray that it didn't budge, even when she shook her head. Several librarians have come and gone since Mrs. Lewis retired, but much of the old, beautiful library is still the same, like the heavy wooden doors, the big marble staircase, and the wonderful smell of books, which Leonard finds very comforting.

After he got his books from the library, he headed over to the grocery store, for the week's provisions:

5 Cup O'Noodles

7 cans Campbell's soup

1 box Quaker Instant oatmeal

Bread

Instant coffee

Quart of milk

Butter

Eggs

American cheese

When Leonard returned home from his errands, his neighbor, Patty, was outside, tending to the pots of flowers she likes to grow on her side of the stoop. Long ago, the two sides of their duplex were identical, mirror images of each other. But that is no longer the case. These days, it is abundantly clear which side of the house is Leonard's and which side is Patty's. Leonard's front door is brown, and unadorned, while Patty's is painted a lovely shade of purple, with a large, colorful wreath that she changes to suit each season. Leonard's side of the stoop has a simple, black rubber doormat in front of the door. Patty's side of the stoop has several pots of colorful flowers on the sides of the steps, and a coir doormat in front of the door, which says "Wipe your paws" along with some jaunty painted paw prints. Leonard's front window has simple, beige blinds, while Patty's front window has floral curtains, along with a large hanging spider plant on the inside, and a large window box, filled with flowers, on the outside.

Leonard smiled and nodded to Patty as he headed toward the stoop with his bags of groceries.

"I can set my watch by you, Leonard." she told him.

Chapter 7

October 12, 2013

Several months after Mrs Lebowitz had headed off to Albany with her daughter, Leonard came home from running errands one Saturday afternoon to find a moving truck parked in front of the duplex. As he approached the steps, he heard laughter and voices coming from the open front door. A middle-aged woman appeared in the doorway, dressed in faded jeans, a Hard Rock Cafe t-shirt, and red Converse All-Stars high-tops.

"Oh, Hi!" She said, as she saw Leonard.

"Hello," replied Leonard, setting his groceries down on the steps..

"You must be my new neighbor! I'm Patty." Said the woman, extending her hand across the railing that divided the stoop.

Leonard nodded, and shook her hand. "I suppose I am. It's nice to meet you, Patty. I'm Leonard."

Just then, a pair of young men appeared, laughing and pushing each other as they came out the front door. They stopped abruptly to avoid bumping into Patty, who raised an eyebrow at them, before breaking into a wide smile. The two young men looked like a matching set, same face, same tousled brown hair, same style of khaki shorts. Only their t-shirts were different... one solid blue, and one with what appeared to be a band logo, which Leonard did not recognize.

"And these two goofballs are my nephews, Max and Caleb." She said, "They're home from college to help their Auntie unload the truck."

The boys said hello before bouncing down the steps and back to the truck.

"And yes... they're twins." She laughed. "Everyone always asks."

"I figured," said Leonard. "They look alike."

"Yup. Identical. My sister, Bonnie, their mother, used to paint Max's toenail so she could tell them apart. Now it's easy. Caleb's the one with a scar on his chin, from when Max dared him to jump from the top bunk when they were six. Boys..." she sighed, shaking her head.

Just then, a large fluffy dog came bounding up the walkway, wagging his tail and barking, followed by a woman who looked like a slightly smaller, blonde version of Patty, and a young girl, who was holding on to the end of the leash. The dog ran right up to Patty.

"Barney!" She exclaimed, bending down to greet the dog. "And this is Barney, my dog. And my sister Kelly, and my niece, Sophie..."

"Hello." Said Leonard, feeling slightly overwhelmed by all this commotion. At this point, he was rather unclear as to exactly how many of these people dashing about were actually going to live here, and how many were just helping with the move.

"I'm FIVE," said Sophie, holding her outstretched fingers up toward Leonard. "How old are you?"

"Oh!" Leonard was caught off guard a bit, as he was unaccustomed to being spoken to by children. "Uh, I'm Fifty-five."

The boys were on their way up the steps with a large bookcase, so with a "Nice to meet you," Kelly and Sophie headed inside with the dog, to get out of the way, and Patty pointed into the house.

"That's going in the living room, boys. Thanks." She turned to Leonard. "Well, it's good to meet you, Leonard. This seems like a very nice neighborhood. I think we're going to like it here."

Leonard nodded. Small talk did not come easily to him. "Yes." He said. "It is, I mean, a nice neighborhood. I like it."

The boys came bounding back down the steps and out to the truck. "These two..." Patty smiled, shaking her head. "Well, better get back to it," she said, pointing toward the truck. "I promised them all pizza when we're done. See you around!"

Leonard nodded and waved, then unlocked his door. He had been wondering who had bought the condo, and had been hoping they would be nice. Patty and her family did, indeed, seem very nice, and definitely did not seem like the sort of people who would shout angrily out the window, so Leonard was grateful for that.

Chapter 8

October 15, 2013

"Welcome to Fernando's!" Said the hostess. "How many in your party?"

"PATTY!! OVER HERE!" Patty and the hostess both turned toward the voice, coming from a large table in the corner of the dining room, surrounded by balloons and an enthusiastic group of smiling, waving people.

"I'm with them," Patty said, sheepishly, pointing in their direction.

As Patty approached the table, her two younger sisters, Bonnie and Kelly, jumped up to hug her, followed by her twin nephews, her niece, and her brother-in-law, all of them wishing her a Happy Birthday.

Her eighty-year-old father isn't able to jump up these days, so Patty went over to his seat at the end of the table to hug him, then settled herself into the empty chair next to him.

Patty noticed there was a glitter-encrusted sign sticking out of the floral bouquet on the table that said "50 and FABULOUS!"

"Aw, thanks. You sure do know how to make an old lady feel special."

"What's this 'old lady' nonsense." Said Patty's father. "You're just a baby."

"Oh Dad..." said Patty, as the server came over to take their drink orders.

"Aren't you going to check her ID?" Patty's Dad asked the server with a wink.

"So, Patty... what's it like to be a half-century old?" Asked Kelly, Patty's youngest sister, from the other end of the table.

Patty laughed, and shook her head. "Ooh, boy... it's been a wild ride, for sure. I mean, if you'd told the younger version of me that I'd be in the middle of a divorce, and moving into a new home of my own, the very same week I celebrated my fiftieth birthday, I would not have believed it. But here I am!" She shrugged, and took a sip of her wine.

"You're going to make it through just fine, Patty-cake." Said her father. "You're strong, like your mother. She'd be so proud of you."

"Thank you, Dad." She said, reaching over to squeeze his hand. "I have to say, I'm so much happier than I have been in many years."

"We love you, Goober," Bonnie said. "And I think I speak for all of us, when I say that I am looking forward to a Todd-free holiday season!"

"Here, here!" Said Patty, raising her glass.

"How are you liking the new place?" Asked Nick, Bonnie's husband, as their entrees arrived.

"I love it! I plan to do some repainting, and I still have so much unpacking to do, but I think Barney and I are going to be very happy there. It's starting to feel like home."

26

Chapter 9

October 1943

After Earl and Florence returned from their honeymoon in The Poconos, they lived with Florence's parents for a few months, until they were able to get a place of their own. It didn't take long for them to find the perfect home in which to start their family: an adorable ranch-style house, built only a few years earlier. It was on the small side, but the lot was plenty big enough to expand as their family grew.

The house sat on a quiet, tree-lined side street. It had a small front lawn with a flag stone walkway leading up to the house. There were rose trellises on either side of the front steps, along with yew and boxwood shrubs. The living room had a big picture window, and a brick fireplace at one end. There was a spacious, eat-in kitchen, and a hallway led to two large bedrooms, and a bathroom with mint green tiles. Out through the kitchen door was a large, fenced-in backyard, with an apple tree, an abandoned vegetable patch, and, in the back corner, a large maple tree. It was only the second house they'd looked at, but the moment they saw it, Florence squeezed Earl's hand and whispered. "I think this is our home."

The night after they'd signed the purchase and sale agreement, they lay side by side in the dark, talking about how wonderful it was going to be to have a home that was all their own. They imagined the beautiful future they would create there together.

"I can't wait to be looking out that kitchen window as our children play in the yard," said Florence, snuggling into Earl's chest. "And we'll pick apples for pies, and we'll plant a big vegetable garden!"

Earl wrapped his arms around his wife, and kissed the top of her head.

"I could hang a tire swing from that big maple tree. Children should definitely have a tire swing."

"Yes!" Exclaimed Florence. "And in the winter, we can all sit by the fireplace, to read and talk after dinner."

After they moved into the new house, Florence settled easily into her new role as a homemaker. Every morning, she made the coffee, prepared breakfast for her husband and packed his lunchbox while he was getting himself ready for work. After she kissed him goodbye, she kept herself busy with turning their new house into a home. She hung pictures on the walls, crocheted doilies and sewed curtains. She took great pride in their home, which was always scrubbed spotlessly clean, and filled with the delicious scent of a home-cooked dinner by the time Earl came home from work each day at 5:45pm.

While she was cooking, cleaning and decorating their new home, she was also hoping that the stork might pay them a visit. Because more than anything else in the world, Florence wanted to be a mother. It had been her dream since she was just a small child herself. She and her sister Eleanor were always playing with dolls when they were young girls, and they'd talk for hours about how many children they would have one day, and what they would name those future children.

Florence thought for sure that she and Earl would have a baby by the time their first wedding anniversary arrived, but this was not the case. Her sister Eleanor had given birth to her first baby, Jimmy, just ten months after her wedding, and her youngest, Nancy, came along three years later. Most of the girls she knew from school had also gotten pregnant very soon after their weddings. And although Florence would certainly never gossip, she suspected that some of the girls might have been expecting before their weddings, given the number of "premature" babies she knew of who arrived as plump, 8-pound cherubs.

Florence thought about her teenage years, when she'd been warned, repeatedly, that a girl had best just keep her legs crossed until after marriage, because having sex would most certainly lead to pregnancy. But since their wedding, Florence and Earl had been having plenty of sex, as newlyweds do, and yet, none of it had gotten her pregnant. Earl reassured her that it was probably just because it had been a hectic year, what with buying the new house and all.

"Sometimes these things take time," he told her. "I'm sure it will happen soon enough."

But by their second wedding anniversary, they were still waiting for a baby. Florence had tried every trick in the book. Her mother told her to drink warm milk every night, and the old woman next door told her to have a spoonful of honey and cinnamon every morning. She put charms under her pillow, and she drank special tea. But every 28 days, like clockwork, she found herself very definitely not pregnant.

To celebrate their third wedding anniversary, Earl surprised Florence with a romantic weekend getaway by the shore. He'd found a cute little motel, which boasted ocean views from every room. Surely, a relaxing weekend, breathing in some fresh sea air, would help to bring on a pregnancy. It was a lovely weekend, and they had the most wonderful time. They spent two days relaxing on the beach, and two nights making love to the sound of waves crashing onto the shore from the open window of their motel room. On the drive home from the shore, they stopped to browse some antique shops. In one of those shops, they found an antique carved wood cradle. It was covered in dust, and had quite a few scratches, but it was well-made, and they could see that with a bit of work it would be absolutely beautiful. Over the next few weekends, Earl cleaned it up, and sanded and polished it to a lustrous shine, while Florence sewed a small bedding set, of buttery yellow cotton.

Chapter 10

2018

Leonard always feels a bit melancholy on Sundays. There is a heaviness in his limbs, and a vague hollow feeling in his chest. But he's not one to dwell on such things; he doesn't see the point in doing so. He prefers to just "keep on keeping on," as he's heard the younger people at work say.

He manages to keep his ennui at bay by maintaining his usual habits: he always wakes up at 6:30am, and then, as usual, he showers, shaves, and gets dressed in chinos and a crisply ironed cotton shirt. Once he's dressed for the day, he retrieves the Sunday newspaper from the front stoop. Since he doesn't have to get out to catch the bus on Sundays, he always has a leisurely breakfast, of soft boiled egg with toast, while he does the Sunday crossword puzzle. When the last bit of runny yolk has been mopped up with the last crust of buttery toast, he always makes sure his breakfast dishes are washed, dried and put away, because his dear mother, God rest her soul, always said, "A tidy home is a happy home." Then, he always pours himself a second cup of coffee to enjoy while he reads through the rest of the Sunday paper.

At 12:30pm, he always fixes himself a grilled cheese sandwich and some Campbell's tomato soup for lunch, just like his dear mother, God rest her soul, used to make. Then, he goes out for a nice, long walk. He has come to rely on the peace and comfort that this long Sunday walk offers him. Leonard doesn't own a fitness tracker, of course, but if he did, it would clock 3.7 miles of walking, every Sunday afternoon.

When he returns home again, he always makes himself a cup of tea. Leonard always buys Salada tea, the same brand his dear mother, God rest her soul, always used to buy. Salada was her favorite brand, because she loved the little sayings printed on the tea bag tags. To this day, when Leonard reads the tea bag tag quotes to himself, he hears his mother's voice saying them.

At 5:45pm, he always has Campbell's Chicken Noodle soup for dinner. After dinner, Leonard always relaxes in the living room with a good book, then goes to bed at 9pm on the dot.

Chapter 11

July 1948

As the occasion of their fifth wedding anniversary approached, Florence had just turned thirty-two, and there were still no babies. She found herself experiencing a painful pang of jealousy when she saw pregnant women at the market, or young mothers pushing baby carriages down the street. It's not that she begrudged those women their happiness; that simply wasn't Florence's way. She just desperately wanted to have a chance at that happiness, too.

One Sunday afternoon, there had been an unfortunate incident during dinner at Florence's parents' house, which pushed the typically brave-faced Florence right over the edge. The whole family was there, Dr and Mrs Anderson, Eleanor, her husband, and their two children, and Earl and Florence. They sat around the large, oval, mahogany dining room table, plates filled with roast beef, mashed potatoes and peas with pearl onions.

"Please pass the gravy, Alice..." Florence's father asked his wife.

"Of course, Dear," Alice replied, passing the silver gravy boat to her husband. "I meant to tell you, Eleanor... the other day I was at Pearson's Pharmacy, and I ran into that red-haired girl you went to school with, Ellen,"

"It's Helen," said Eleanor, buttering a roll.

"Right, Helen. Anyway, she's having another baby... any day now. It's her ninth, if you can believe it. Her last baby isn't even a year old, yet! Those Catholics, I tell you..."

Although Florence did her best to hide it, Eleanor caught the little flash of sadness that drifted across her sister's face, before she forced a small smile.

"Mom," said Eleanor.

But Alice kept going. "I just can't even imagine how those women manage. I mean, the Flanigans, next door, with eleven children? Doris was just telling me last week, that now that all her children are having children, she can hardly even keep track of how many grandkids there are!"

Eleanor and Florence exchanged a look, and Earl squeezed Florence's hand under the table.

"Now if I remember correctly, Ann Marie was in your class, Florence, wasn't she?" Alice continued, as she cut into her slice of roast beef. "Anyway, Doris was just telling me that Ann Marie went to the hospital to have her fifth baby. She already has those four boys, and the whole family was convinced she'd have another boy. But, she got quite a surprise, because it turns out, it was twins! A boy... and a girl."

"More gravy, Dad?" Said Florence, a bit more shrilly than she had intended. She stood, picking up the gravy boat as she did, and headed to the kitchen.

"Mother, honestly." Whispered Eleanor, as Earl got up to follow his wife.

"What? Alice asked, innocently. "What's wrong with Florence?".

"Mother," whispered Eleanor, "you know that babies are a difficult subject for her these days."

Alice let out a dramatic breath. "Oh, I see... so we can't ever talk about babies again, just because Florence is barren?"

At the loud "CLANG-SPLAT" sound of the full gravy boat hitting the floor, they all turned toward the doorway to the kitchen.

On the ride home, Florence sobbed in the passenger seat, while Earl tried to reassure her that she was not, as her mother said, "barren." He suggested that maybe, it might be a good idea to talk to a doctor, just to see what's going on. So Florence made an appointment with their family doctor, and the following week she was given a thorough physical examination, along with some blood tests. The doctor found Florence to be perfectly healthy, and couldn't find any physical reason as to why she had been unable to conceive.

"Well, Mrs Thompson, sometimes the problem is up here," the doctor told her, tapping his graying his temple with his index finger. "You just need to relax. Maybe you should take up smoking."

Florence found it to be a bit insulting to be told that her inability to conceive was all in her head. She was plenty relaxed. Besides, taking up smoking was not an option for her. The smell of cigarette smoke made her feel queasy, and her husband was asthmatic.

No knowing what else to do, Earl and Florence went to church, and they prayed for God to bless them with a child. When her period came again, right on schedule, as it always did, Florence began slipping out to the church every morning after Earl left for work, to sit alone in the sanctuary, light candles and pray to be blessed with a child. She was anxiously hopeful for twenty-three days of each month, then cried bitter tears for five days. Earl didn't know what to do. He also looked forward to having children, but he understood that it was very different for Florence. She was desperate to be a mother. It broke his heart to see her so sad.

Chapter 12

August 4, 2018

It was just before 8:00am when Patty finished loading up the car with the cooler, towels, beach chairs and blanket. She checked to make sure she remembered to toss her sunscreen into her bag, then pulled out her iPhone, and sent a text to Bonnie and Kelly:

"Get ready, Bitches! Annual Sisters Beach Day is ON! Leaving now."

Every August, Patty, Bonnie and Kelly would drive out the the beach, just the three of them. It was one of her favorite traditions they had together.

Patty and her two sisters were all born within a span of five years, so they'd grown up very close. They bickered as teenagers, of course, over who stole whose clothes, or who was hogging the bathroom, but the bond they shared was undeniable; each sister would go to battle with anyone who dared mess with one of the other sisters.

The three sisters had all taken different paths in life. Patty had always wanted to be a nurse, and in typical first-born fashion, had been driven in her pursuit of her career. She married Todd, in spite of a good number of red flags, in the hope of also having a happy home life, but that hadn't gone so well. Patty often wondered if maybe she'd been too optimistic, to think she could have both a satisfying career and a happy marriage.

Bonnie, the middle sister, had met her husband, Nick, at the age of 20, at the community college where she studied Early Childhood Education. After graduation, she worked as a preschool teacher, while Nick went on to get a computer science degree. They married in their mid-twenties, and bought a house a couple of years after that. When the twins came along, Bonnie became stay-at-home mother. For many years, her life revolved around play groups, little league, Cub Scouts, music lessons and soccer camps, and she loved it. Her marriage isn't perfect. Nick leaves little hairs in the bathroom sink when he shaves, and he has terrible taste in movies, and Bonnie tends to overthink everything, which drives Nick crazy. Yet, after all this time, they are still in love, and Bonnie knows that is a rare and wonderful thing.

Kelly, the youngest, had been the rebellious one in the family. Their mother had nearly fainted when, at the age of 17, she came home with a large butterfly tattooed on her lower back, and she'd once been suspended from high school for a week, for distributing a zine which called out the school's sexist dress code policies. As an adult, Kelly had found a career doing publicity and fundraising for a variety of non-profits and charitable organizations. She hadn't been particularly interested in marrying any of the men she'd dated, but she did want to be a mother. So as her thirty-ninth birthday approached, she found a sperm donor. The night that Sophie was born was the best night of Kelly's life. She was surrounded by her two sisters, and as the midwife placed her precious baby on her chest, Patty and Bonnie sang "Isn't She Lovely" by Stevie Wonder and they all cried.

Patty picked up Bonnie first, and then Kelly, and then they got onto the highway for the two hour-ride to the beach. The ride to and from the beach was Patty's favorite part of Sisters Beach Day. They'd blast 80's music, gossip, pass snacks around, and laugh until their faces hurt. Then, after they'd gotten too much sun and their hair was crispy with salt water, they'd do the same thing on the ride home. It was the best. Patty loved those two women with her whole heart.

Chapter 13

June 1951

"Remember when we were small? We thought we'd marry princes and have six children each." Florence was hulling and slicing a bowl of strawberries at Eleanor's kitchen table, while her sister was setting sterilized canning jars out on a tea towel.

Eleanor laughed. "Of course I remember. I don't think we considered how difficult it would be to go about finding a prince in Massachusetts. We did alright, though. James and Earl might not be princes, but I suspect marrying royalty comes with its own set of problems."

"True," Florence replied.

Eleanor could tell by the wistful expression on her sister's face that she was really thinking about the "children" part of their unrealized girlhood dream. Back then, pushing doll carriages around the neighborhood, they'd taken for granted that they'd grow up and simply have as many children as they wanted. But it hadn't worked out that way. Eleanor had gotten pregnant easily. She had Jimmy, and was pregnant again a year later, though that pregnancy ended in a miscarriage, which broke her heart. Her sweet little Nancy came along soon after, but there had been complications after Nancy's birth, and a surgery. So she and James were parents of two, not six. But Florence...well, poor Florence.

"I've been thinking," Florence, said, as she poured the berries into a large pot, "about how I planned my whole life around the idea of being a mother. And, for eight years now, I've just been waiting for that life to start. I'm thirty-five years old already." Her voice trembled. "Maybe I've been waiting for the wrong thing?"

"Oh Florence," Eleanor said, as she hugged her sister.

"I mean, if it was meant to be, it would have happened. Don't you think?" Florence accepted the hanky that Eleanor handed her, and wiped her tears. "But it hasn't. We've done everything that we're supposed to do, and it still hasn't happened."

Eleanor didn't know what to say. She was so grateful that she had been able to have a family. But also, because she loved Florence so, she felt guilty that she had been blessed with children, while her sister had not. It wasn't fair. Eleanor didn't deserve it more Florence. She just got lucky.

They stood together in silence, as Florence stirred the pot of strawberries, both of them deep in thought.

"Fluffy..." Eleanor said at last, calling her sister by her childhood nickname. "I don't know what is or isn't meant to be. I wish I did, but I don't. I just know that even if you were a mother, that wouldn't even be the best thing about you. You're already the best sister, aunt, daughter, wife and friend. You are a woman of many talents, and honestly, the smartest person I know."

"Oh, Elmer. I don't deserve you." Florence dabbed her eyes with a hanky.

"It's all true."

41

"Well," Florence took a deep breath. "I've finally accepted it. I'm not going to be mother. And, I love Earl so much, and I love being his wife, but... what now?"

"Whatever you do, you're going to be the best at it. Unless it's making jam, because that pot's about to boil over."

Florence squealed, and moved the pot off the burner. Once the berries were safe, she turned back to Eleanor.

"What would I do without you?"

"Well," replied Eleanor. "You're stuck with me, so you're never going to have to find out."

Florence laughed. "Thank goodness for that."

Chapter 14

August 6, 2018

As Leonard hit "send" on the email he'd just finished, he noticed the time on the corner of his computer screen: 11:59am. He closed his mail program, opened his bottom left desk drawer, and pulled out a Cup O'Noodles. Then he headed down the hallway to the break room, closing his office door behind him.

The break room is located in the center of the building; a large, windowless, square room, with four rectangular tables in the middle, and a kitchenette off to one side. It has not been updated since Leonard first started working at Meyer & Son, back in 1981. The employees at Meyer & Son Manufacturing often complain about its shabby condition. Leonard, however, hadn't really given it much thought until his coworkers began complaining about the scuffed, outdated flooring, the mismatched chairs, or the faint, lingering odor, reminiscent of an elementary school cafeteria. He had just sort of gotten used to it, and had barely noticed its deterioration over the last thirty-seven years, much like the proverbial frog in the pot of water.

As Leonard walked in to the break room, Joan and Carrie from Customer Service were sitting at the table by the door, and Mike,

Kevin, and Jim from Shipping and Receiving were sitting at the table closest to the kitchenette.

"Hi, Leonard," said Joan, as Carrie gave him a friendly wave. "How's it going?"

"Can't complain," said Leonard, as he microwaved the water for his soup.

He sees that there are now two laminated paper signs taped to the microwave. One of them has been there for years. It has a drawing of a fish on a plate, with x's for eyes, and says:

Before You Microwave:
THINK!
DOES IT STINK?

The other sign is new. It doesn't have any drawings. It just says:

DO NOT MICROWAVE METAL!!!!

Leonard wondered what may have transpired in the last twenty-four hours to necessitate the addition of this new sign.

"Cup O'Noodles again, Leonard?" Said Mike, shaking his head.

Kevin and Jim snickered. Leonard shrugged.

Mike, egged on by the snickering, continued. "Geez, have you ever eaten anything else for lunch?"

"Yes, of course." said Leonard, "On Saturdays I have a peanut butter and jelly sandwich, and on Sundays I have a grilled cheese sandwich and tomato soup."

Mike, Kevin and Jim all laughed, but Leonard didn't know what was funny.

"You sure are something," said Mike.

"Look who's talking, Mike," called Carrie. "You're over there shoving a ham and cheese into your pie hole every day for the last two years, and no one's bothering you about it."

Chapter 15

July 1951

Florence decided that it was time to make some changes in her life. She had given the matter a great deal of thought since her conversation with Eleanor. So when Earl came down for breakfast, she set his coffee, eggs and toast on the table, then sat down in the chair across from him.

"Earl," she said. "I've had a realization."

Earl stopped unfolding the paper, and looked at her expectantly. "You have? About what?"

Florence took a deep breath, then began. "We've been trying to have a baby for eight years now, and I haven't even had so much as a missed period."

Earl set the paper down on the table. "Yes," he said sadly, and nodded to her to continue.

And, well, I think that maybe God has been trying to tell me something." Her voice began to quiver as tears welled up in her eyes. "It isn't going to happen for us. I'm just not meant to be a mother..."

"Oh... " said Earl, as he reached toward her. "Oh, Sweetheart. Come here."

Florence sat on his lap, and sobbed as he wrapped his arms around her. When she was able to speak again, she sniffled, "I think I've been so focused on trying to get pregnant that maybe I've missed what I'm supposed to do? Maybe there's something else out there for me?"

Earl just held her in his arms, slowly breathing in the scent of her floral perfume. Then, he swallowed his own tears, and whispered into her hair. "I love you more than anything, Florence Thompson... and the only thing that matters to me is that you're happy. So, whatever you want or need... well, I'll do anything to make you happy."

Florence nodded silently, kissed her husband, and then got up to wash the skillet.

Once they had accepted their fate, and made the conscious decision to be content as a family of two, Florence and Earl Thompson began the next chapter of their lives. That very same morning, after she handed Earl his lunchbox and kissed him goodbye, she dropped the antique cradle off at St. Luke's for the annual church rummage sale. Then, she came home and set to work, turning the room they'd hoped would be a nursery into a study for her dear husband. That evening, she cooked Earl's favorite pot roast for dinner, which she served by candlelight.

A few weeks later, Florence found herself a job, as a secretary at the elementary school around the corner from their house. She found that she really enjoyed working at the school. It got her out of the house and gave her something interesting and useful to do with her time. She found the school to be a much more cheerful work environment than her old job, at Randall & Bernstein's accounting firm. Mrs Thompson, the school secretary, soon became a well-known, friendly face at the school. The children always waved and said hello to her as they passed by the front office. She was also known for keeping a little glass bowl of butterscotch candy on her desk, in case a student (or a teacher) was having a bad day, and needed a little bit of cheering up.

Even with her new job, Florence was still home by 3pm every afternoon, to take care of the house and prepare dinner, which was, as always, on the table when Earl arrived home from work at 5:45pm. On Fridays, Earl stopped on his way home to buy a bouquet of fresh flowers for Florence, which she'd place in a vase on the table. They had Sunday dinners with the Andersons, played bridge with the neighbors, and went on a vacation to the shore every summer. The life they settled into wasn't the one they had planned on, but still, it was a comfortable, pleasant life.

Life, however, can be wildly unpredictable. As Christmas of 1957 approached, Florence had begun to feel unwell. Earl was terribly concerned, but Florence insisted she was just tired from the Christmas shopping, and baking all those sugar cookies for the school's holiday party.

"With a little rest, I'll be right as rain." She told him.

But over the next few days, her fatigue only increased, and she began to suffer bouts of dizziness and nausea. When Florence fainted in the kitchen, on New Year's Day, Earl called for an ambulance.

Chapter 16

August 6, 2018

After he finished his lunch, Leonard headed back down the hall to his office. He sat down at his desk, and took out his agenda to check his afternoon meeting schedule. He opened it to the current page and saw he had just one meeting scheduled for today: Margaret Olson, at 2pm. Leonard smiled. He liked Margaret, who was one of only a few employees left in the company who were older than him. She had always been kind to him. When his dear mother, God rest her soul, passed away in 1994, Margaret dropped off several casseroles to Leonard's home, and that Christmas, she and her husband, Carl, invited him to join their family for dinner. He declined the offer, as he didn't wish to be a burden, but he often thinks back to that kind gesture. And when Leonard received his plaque for twenty-five years of service to Meyer & Son Manufacturing, back in 2006, Margaret had baked him a carrot cake, his favorite, which was a very thoughtful thing to do.

At 2pm on the nose, there was a tap on his office door. That's another thing he has always appreciated about Margaret Olson. She is always punctual.

"Hello, Leonard," she said as she sits in the chair across from the desk.

"It's good to see you, Margaret," he replied, straightening the papers on his desk. "How can I help you today?"

Margaret sighed, and a serene smile spread across her face. "Well, I'm finally retiring, if you can believe it!"

"Retiring! Wow. That's something."

"Yes. Carl retired last year, and, well, it just feels like the right time. I'm looking forward to having more time with the grandkids. My youngest, Tommy, and his wife are expecting again."

"Oh, how nice. Congratulations." Said Leonard.

"Thank you! This will be my fifth grandchild! So, Mr. Meyers will have to make do without me." She said with a wink. "Hard to believe I've been here for twenty-six years already. It sure does fly by..."

Leonard nodded "It sure does.".

"Now, I know I don't need to tell you that," said Margaret. "You've been here even longer than I have!"

Leonard cleared his throat. "Yes, um, I've been here thirty-seven years, now."

Margaret laughed. "You must have been a baby when you started!"

"Um, well... I was twenty-two... started here right after college."

"Well, I think that's impressive."

Leonard smiled awkwardly, and shrugged.

Margaret continued, "Anyway...I'll be here until the 17th, then Carl and I are taking the RV to Vermont for the rest of August, to celebrate that we're both finally retired."

"That sounds wonderful, Margaret." He picked up a pen and a

notepad. "I'll send a note to Mary Beth... the new HR manager?"

"Oh Leonard," said Margaret, smiling. "She's been here almost a year now... that's not so new..."

Leonard cleared his throat again. "Right. Of course. Well, there's some paperwork for you... for the 401k and such... Mary Beth handles that..."

"Oh, no worries, Leonard... I'll just send an email over." She said, standing up. "Well then, I better get back to work.

"Alrighty," said Leonard. "Let me know if there's anything else I can do for you."

She smiled warmly. "Will do. It is always a pleasure talking to you, Leonard."

Leonard waved his goodbye, and as the door closed, he took out his agenda and made a small red check mark next to the meeting entry.

Chapter 17

January 1, 1958

Florence was whisked away to the hospital via Ambulance, while Earl followed behind in their Buick, white knuckled and sweating. Florence, who did not like to be a bother, was terribly embarrassed to have caused such a scene. At the hospital, she was poked and prodded; a battery of tests were run. All the while Florence apologized to everyone for the inconvenience, as was her way. Earl paced the floors of the hospital, attempting to hide his worry, until a doctor with a clip board finally came back, with a diagnosis.

It seemed that Florence Thompson had come down with a case of pregnancy.

Upon hearing the news of their positive pregnancy test, Florence burst into happy tears, while Earl fainted; his tall, lanky frame collapsing in a heap. He was revived quickly, and once it was determined that the poor fellow hadn't sustained any serious injuries when he landed on the floor, a kindly nurse escorted him outside to get some fresh air.

"I am just so sorry about my husband." Florence said the doctor with the clip board. "This is, well, this is a bit of a surprise, to say the least." She dabbed at her tears with her handkerchief. Her heart was practically bursting with joy.

"It happens more often than you might expect. We get a fainting father at least once a week, around here." the doctor said, with a wry smile. Then he cleared his throat, and pulled a pen from the pocket of his white jacket.

"Well, Mrs Thompson, with a positive pregnancy test, we're going to need to determine how far along your pregnancy might be, to estimate when the baby might be due. So let's start with... when was your last menstrual cycle?"

"Hmm, let's see," said Florence, trying to remember. "I guess it was maybe, October?"

The doctor looked at her with surprise. "So, Mrs. Thompson," He stamped his cigarette out in the ashtray on his desk. "You're saying that you've missed at least two menstrual cycles? I'm surprised you didn't... well..."

"Yes, I know... But, well, I didn't think it was possible!" Exclaimed Florence, laughing through tears. "We tried for years and years to have a baby, but it never happened. I thought I was barren! I'm almost 43, so, when I didn't get my monthly, I thought I was just going through The Change!"

It was determined that their baby would arrive in July. To finally be pregnant, after so many years with an empty womb, Florence knew with absolute certainty that she had been been touched by a miracle.

As they drove home from the hospital on that cold January day, she could not contain her overflowing heart.

"A baby!" She kept saying, over and over. "Earl! Can you believe it?! We made a baby!"

Earl just shook his head. He was still in shock.

Florence was so excited to share their good news with Eleanor, and the rest of the family. As soon as they got home, she went straight to the phone in the kitchen and started dialing. To say that everyone was surprised would be an understatement, but they were also so happy to hear there would be a new little one in the family. And, of course, they were thrilled that Florence would finally get to be a mother, as she'd always dreamed. Florence only wished that her father were still here, to share in this joyful event. He'd passed away just a year before, of lung cancer.

The next morning, Eleanor stopped by Florence and Earl's house, carrying a white box, which contained the family Christening gown. Their mother had worn it when she was Christened more than sixty five years ago. Florence and Eleanor had each worn it for their Christenings, as had both of Eleanor's children. Now, Earl and Florence's baby would get to wear it. Florence lifted the gown from the layers of tissue paper, where it had sat since Nancy's Christening seventeen years earlier. As Florence touched the delicate lace trim, tears welled up in her eyes.

By the end of the week, Florence handed Earl a list of all the things they would need to get before the baby arrived. She spent her evenings knitting blankets and sweaters and booties, as she and Earl discussed baby names, and the dreams they shared for their child. As her belly grew, they'd lie in bed at night, Earl's hands on the big, round ball of her tummy, and sing to the baby, both of them delighted by every little poke and kick.

After they'd purchased a crib, bureau, changing table and rocking chair from the Sears & Roebuck catalog, Earl's desk was moved into the living room, and his study was transformed into the nursery they'd always hoped it would be. Earl hung the wallpaper that Florence had chosen, which was a lovely pale green, scattered with adorable yellow bunnies and little white flowers. Florence hummed as she sewed yellow gingham curtains for the nursery windows. Earl had always heard people say that women had a "glow" about them when they were expecting, but up until now, he hadn't really understood what that meant. But for the rest of his life he will remember the joyful light that radiated from his wife during those months. She was the happiest he'd ever seen her, and she was more beautiful than ever.

Chapter 18

July 15, 1958

Florence was standing in the kitchen, scooping mashed potatoes into a serving bowl, when her water broke. Earl walked in from work to find her standing there in a puddle, eyes like saucers, with the serving spoon still in her hand. For several weeks, they'd been preparing for the big event, making lists, washing and stacking piles of diapers, and sterilizing bottles. For weeks, Florence's bag for the hospital had been packed and sitting by the front door, ready to go when the time came. However, they had not accounted for the water breaking, so some minor adjustments needed to be made to their plan. Earl gathered some bath towels to put down on the seat of the Buick, while Florence stashed the dinner food in the fridge. Then, Earl helped his wife into the car.

When they arrived at the hospital, Florence was whisked away in a wheelchair, and Earl was shown to a waiting room, where two other men were also waiting. One of the men, who looked to be in his mid-twenties, was pacing back and forth across the room, wringing his hands. Another, who looked to be of a similar age, sat in a chair next to a very full ashtray, smoking and tapping his foot. Earl wasn't quite sure what to do with himself. He wasn't a smoker, so he followed the other fellow's lead and started pacing. After they'd nearly collided a couple of times, Earl sat down and picked up a magazine from the table next to him. He was too nervous to read, so he just flipped through the pages.

By the time Earl was on his fourth magazine, the pacing man was approached by a nurse, who informed him that he was the father of a new baby girl. Earl and the smoker congratulated him, as he followed the nurse down to the nursery to see his new daughter. Earl took a deep breath, and settled in with another magazine, this one a six-month-old issue of *Popular Mechanics*.

"Mr. Thompson?" Earl jumped to his feet, nearly knocking over the chair he'd been sitting in. "It's a boy, Mr. Thompson." Said a nurse. "Mother and Baby are doing just fine."

When Leonard was born, his mother was forty-three years old, and his father was forty-five. They'd been married for fifteen childless years, and had long ago given up any hope of being parents. Leonard was their Little Miracle, which his mother reminded him of nearly every day. Florence was the very definition of a doting mother. She loved Leonard beyond measure, and was completely devoted to his comfort and care. Earl also loved his son, but he was of the generation of fathers who weren't particularly involved in child rearing. He had been raised with the understanding that babies were the domain of mothers, so he did his best to keep out of the way until Leonard was old enough to talk. Even then, he wasn't one to be particularly demonstrative; he showed his affection with the occasional "Atta boy" and a pat on the back.

As Leonard grew, he began to notice that his parents were quite a bit older than the parents of the other children who lived in the neighborhood. It was fairly common for strangers to mistake them for his grandparents. The first time he remembers this happening, he was about five years old. He'd gone out to the hardware store with his Dad, to get some nails and paint to repair their fence, which had been damaged when a tree limb fell during a storm. The man behind the counter gave Leonard a lollipop, and told him that he was such a good boy to be helping his Grandpa fix the fence. This was very confusing to Leonard, since, to his knowledge, he didn't have a Grandpa. The only grandparent he had was Grandma Alice, his mother's mother, who kept her teeth in a glass next to her bed. Which, by the way, was another thing that Leonard found quite confusing.

Chapter 19

August 16, 2018

It was late morning on a Wednesday, and Leonard was sitting at his desk at Meyer & Son, adding a new hire into the payroll system, when there was a quick rhythmic knock on his office door. Leonard was startled. He hadn't been expecting anyone. He looked up to see the door open a crack, and Mary Beth's blond hair and meticulously made-up, smiling face peered around the door.

"Knock knock!" She said in her cheerful, sing-song voice. "Got a minute, Leonard?"

"Oh." Said Leonard, turning his attention from his computer to Mary Beth. "Yes, of course... what can I do for you?"

MaryBeth held out a large greeting card and a pen to Leonard. "It's a card, for Margaret."

"Oh, well, that's nice." Said Leonard, taking the card from her. There was a picture of a fluffy white dog lying on a beach chair, wearing a bandana and heart-shaped sunglasses, and it said, "Congratulations on your Retirement!" He wondered why people seemed to find it amusing to put costumes on dogs. Leonard thought it must be terribly embarrassing for the poor dogs. He signed the card, and handed it,and the pen, back to Mary Beth.

"Thank you!" She sang. "Oh, and just one more thing... I wanted to touch base, because... Do you know that you have a ton of PTO built up?"

"Oh, that. yes." Leonard nodded.

"Yeah, so," Mary Beth sat down in the chair across from his desk. "Um, if you don't take it, like, by the end of the year, well... it won't carry over..."

"Yes, I know." Leonard replied.

"OK, so... Do you have, like, vacation plans or anything? Because you'll want to get the request in soon, because, you know, how it is, this time of year..." She tapped her French-manicured nails on the desk.

"No, actually, I don't have any plans." Leonard replied.

"Um, OK, but you know that the PTO doesn't carry over. Like, it's 'use it or lose it,' you know? So..." She looked at him expectantly.

She had used those little finger quotes when she said "use it or lose it," a gesture which Leonard has always found to be a bit ridiculous.and yet, it had become ubiquitous in everyday conversation. Leonard just nodded.

Mary Beth stared at him for a moment, then nodded slowly. "Ok, then," she said, standing up. "Well, I better make sure everyone's signed the card."

"Alrighty. Thanks, Mary Beth." Said Leonard with a wave.

Mary Beth closed the door behind her as she left, thinking to herself, "That Leonard is a strange dude. What kind of person doesn't take their PTO?"

Chapter 20

March 1966

Most of Leonard's earliest memories are warm, safe and cozy. He remembers steaming bowls of oatmeal, lovingly prepared by his mother. He remembers the sound of her humming as she puttered about the kitchen. He remembers his father sitting across from him at the breakfast table, doing the crossword puzzle in the morning paper. He remembers walking hand in hand to the library with his mother, returning home with stacks of books they'd read together after supper. He remembers sitting on the floor, counting and sorting the big tin of buttons that his mother let him play with while she was sewing, and the soothing whir of her sewing machine. He remembers homemade birthday cakes, going to get ice cream on summer evenings, and the way his parents always let him choose their Christmas tree from the tree lot down at the VFW. And he remembers lying in bed at night, after he'd been tucked in and given a glass of water, falling asleep to the sound of his parents' quiet voices in the living room.

But things got much harder for Leonard once he started school. For reasons he could never understand, he didn't quite fit in with the other children. They seemed to play together easily, but Leonard was never really sure how to interact with other kids. He always seemed to say the wrong thing, and often the other kids would be laughing about something, but Leonard didn't understand what was so funny. Most kids just ignored him, as if he wasn't even there. There were a few kids who were nice to him, like Amy, a quiet girl who came to their school in second grade, and Ellen, who was the smartest in their class. But then there were some kids who teased Leonard for the thick glasses he wore, and mocked him because he preferred to read his book in the corner of the school yard, rather than play foursquare or tether ball at recess. He was also often teased about his name, which stood out as stuffy and old fashioned in the 1960's and '70's, when the other boys at school had names like Steven, Mark, Michael and Brian. There had been one boy in particular, who was especially cruel to Leonard. His name was Johnny Allen, and he was the ringleader of a group of mean boys, who would torment Leonard for many years.

After school one day, when Leonard was in the third grade, he decided to ask his mother about his name.

"Momma? I have a question. Why did you name me 'Leonard'?"

Florence smiled, as she placed a plate of cookies and a glass of milk in front of her son.

"Oh, I named you after my father, your grandfather, Leonard. He was a wonderful man. I'm sorry you never got to meet him." She noticed her son's furrowed brow. "Why do you ask?"

Leonard took a sip of milk. "Well, some kids at school... they said Leonard is a nerd name..."

Florence sat down across from Leonard, and placed her hand on his. "That is simply not true. Leonard is a wonderful name.

It means "Brave Lion."

"Hm." Said Leonard, as he nodded thoughtfully, and took another bite of his cookie.

"I haven't really told you much about your grandfather, have I?" Asked Florence.

Leonard, his mouth full of cookie, shook his head.

"Well, as I said, he was my father... he was married to Grandma Alice. And he was a brave and wonderful man. He was a doctor, and when I was just a tiny little baby, during The Great War... World War I... he went off to Europe with the Army, to take care of wounded soldiers."

"Wow!" said Leonard. "Was that very dangerous?"

Florence nodded. "Oh, yes, Leonard. It was very dangerous. But it was also very, very important. I was so proud to have him for a father, and I was really sad when he died."

Leonard's eyes grew wide. "Did he die at the war?" He asked.

"Oh, no, sweetheart. He didn't. He came back a year or so later, and then he worked at the hospital for many years, which was much less dangerous. But still very, very important. He died much later, after I was a grown up."

Leonard looked relieved.

She continued, "Your grandfather Leonard worked hard his whole life to take care of people, and that's something very special."

"So that's why you named me Leonard."

"Yes, Sweetheart, that's why."

The next day at school, as the children lined up in the hallway to go to the cafeteria for lunch, Johnny Allen and the rest of the mean boys started mocking Leonard's name again.

Leonard straightened his back, crossed his arms over his chest, and held his head high. "Leonard was my grandfather's name," he told them. "It means Brave Lion."

The bullies burst into laughter at this, though Leonard wasn't sure why. And after that, they started calling him Leonard the Lion, a name that would follow him throughout the rest of his school days. He figured out pretty quickly that it was not meant as a compliment.

The contrast between the stability and safety of his home, and the emotional minefield of school took its toll on Leonard. He began to suffer from anxiety, though in the 1960's, that sort of thing wasn't really recognized. He began complaining of stomach aches in the morning before school, which concerned Florence. She took him to Dr. Asher, the pediatrician, but he couldn't find anything wrong with Leonard physically, other than being a little small for his age, which had always been the case.

"Well, Mrs. Thompson, sometimes kids just pretend to have a stomach ache so they can skip school for the day." Said Dr. Asher, winking at Leonard, who immediately felt his face flush with shame.

Florence was indignant. "With all due respect, Dr. Asher, I do not think that is what is happening here. My son gets all A's and B's at school. His teachers tell me he is a model student. He is very bright, and he loves to read. And he would never lie."

As they were leaving, Leonard reached for his mother's coat sleeve. "Momma?"

She stopped walking, and looked down at her son. "What is it, Sweetheart?"

"I'm not lying, Momma." Tears welled up in his eyes. "My stomach really did hurt."

Florence folded her sweet boy into her arms. "I know. I know it did. It's OK. Let's go home and make you some tea."

Leonard eventually learned to cope with the anxiety of school by developing the habit of counting the cracks in the sidewalk on his way to and from school. He counted from one to three hundred thirteen on the way to school, and then from three hundred thirteen down to one on the way home.

Some of the habits we choose to keep ourselves safe as children, can be very hard to shake in adulthood. Such was the case with the other habit Leonard had adopted as a boy: when out in the world, he kept to himself, stayed as quiet as possible, and didn't let his guard down.

Chapter 21

Friday, August 17, 2018

"Good morning, Sunshine!" Called Karen.

"Good morning." Patty replied, as she opened her locker. "Why are you so cheerful this morning?"

Karen held up her mug. "Third cup of coffee! I highly recommend."

Patty laughed. "No thanks... I'll have to pee 10 minutes into my shift. Hey, are you busy tomorrow? I was supposed to go to the Bruno Mars concert with Bonnie, but now I'm covering Maria's shift. She caught the flu. Want my ticket?"

"Wish I could, but I can't." Said Karen. "We're driving out to Boston for my niece's baby shower. What about your neighbor?"

"Leonard? I can't imagine... I mean... I don't think he really does stuff like that."

"What, listen to Bruno Mars?"

"No... I mean, yes, that also... but no, he doesn't go to concerts... or anything, really. Except work, and like, errands. I worry about him, sometimes, honestly."

"Do you think he's lonely?" Karen asked.

"I don't really know. He was really quiet when I first moved in... kind of shy, I guess. But over time he's opened up. He's friendly toward me, to other neighbors, to people delivering packages. But I've also never seen him have anyone over or anything, and like I said before, he doesn't really go out... like, for fun."

"Maybe he's just an introvert." Karen shrugged.

"Yeah, maybe." Patty thought about her neighbor, and his funny little habit of always coming and going from his condo at the same time, wearing an outfit that varied only in color, and the addition or subtraction of outwear as the season required. There was something about him that was a bit old fashioned, definitely a bit quirky.

"Well," said Karen, glancing down at her watch. "it's about that time..."

"Sure is," said Patty, checking her own watch. "Ready for another exciting day in the ED?"

Chapter 22

September 8, 1971

Leonard had some very good reasons to look forward to starting seventh grade. The elementary school that Leonard attended from kindergarten through the sixth grade was a small school, with only one classroom for each grade. This meant that for the entirety of Leonard's elementary school years, he had to suffer the indignity of being in the same class with Johnny Allen. Every summer, he used to pray that Johnny Allen would be held back, so he'd no longer have to be in the same class with him. But since the teachers didn't particularly enjoy having Johnny in class either, they continued to promote him to the next grade, in spite of his poor academic performance.

Leonard had the same twenty or so children in his class since kindergarten, with the exception of a few kids who moved in or out of town during that time. But in the Junior High School, there would be kids from all four of the elementary schools in town, so Leonard figured he would have a better chance at just blending in. And also, in Junior High, students switched classes for each subject, and they had Honors classes. The academic part of school had always been much easier for Leonard than the social part. He loved books, and was an excellent reader. He was also very good at math. He was glad that he would have the opportunity to take honors classes. His parents were proud that he wanted to challenge himself academically, but he was too embarrassed to tell them the real reason why he wanted to be in honors classes. The truth was, Leonard knew that it was highly unlikely that Johnny Allen, who was not the sharpest knife in the drawer, would ever be in an honors class, so he was very much looking forward to being able to get an education without Johnny's constant bullying.

Leonard's first day of seventh grade started off with English first period, followed by United States History, and then Math, all subjects he enjoyed, and all of which were blissfully free of Johnny Allen and the other bullies from elementary school. Fourth period, however, was gym class, which Leonard never enjoyed. He did not see the appeal of sports, and being forced to engage in such things for gym class was a source of great humiliation for Leonard. He was almost always picked last when teams were chosen, and one time, during a game of Dodge Ball in fourth grade, Johnny Allen had lobbed one of those red balls directly at Leonard's face, breaking his glasses and bloodying his nose. Johnny told the gym teacher it was an accident, but everyone else could see that he had done it on purpose. "Who came up with that stupid, barbaric game, anyway?" thought Leonard to himself, as he sat in the nurse's office, holding a wad of tissues to his nose, while the nurse attempted to tape his glasses back together with a Band-aid. By the end of his elementary school years, Leonard managed to figure out a few tricks to minimize his suffering, such as keeping to the very end of the line at kickball, and praying his team would reach three "outs" before he was up.

On that first day of seventh grade, Leonard was changing into his gym clothes in the locker room when he heard the familiar voice behind him.

"Well... look who it is! It's Leonard the Lion!"

Leonard froze, clutching the t-shirt he was about to put on to his chest. Before he knew what was happening, the T-shirt was ripped from his hands, leaving him standing there in just his gym shorts and socks.

"Hey Jimbo!" Johnny called to one of the other boys, as he scrunched Leonard's shirt into a ball. "Catch!"

Leonard stood there helpless, his skinny arms folded over his bare chest, feeling the heat of his embarrassment rising, as the gaggle of mean boys threw his shirt around the locker room, laughing and shouting in a manner that reminded Leonard of some monkeys he'd seen in a nature documentary on the Public Broadcasting Station. Leonard's t-shirt hit the floor several times, and was stepped on more than once, before being picked up and tossed again, always just out of Leonard's reach. When the locker room door opened and Coach Hocker yelled for the boys to "quit fooling around and get a move on," the shirt was tossed back to Leonard, hitting him in the face before it landed on the floor at his feet. He picked it up and held it up to look at it. The previously white t-shirt was now dirty, wrinkled and stretched out, and there was a tear in the shoulder seam. He didn't have another one, so he pulled the shirt over his head, and wiped his tears on the back of his hand.

As he headed out to the gymnasium behind the rest of the class, he thought about how back in fifth grade, he'd missed three months of gym when he'd fractured his arm falling out of the apple tree in his backyard. He remembers clutching the doctor's note he'd been given after they'd put the cast on his arm, giddy at the prospect of being excused from physical education. For those three months, he'd been allowed to spend the whole forty-five minutes of gym class in the school library, instead of the gymnasium, which was wonderful. He wondered if there was a less painful injury he might be able to acquire to get him out of gym class again.

As soon as gym class was over, Leonard hid in a bathroom stall until the locker room was empty. Next period was lunch, so no one else would be coming into the locker room for a bit. He changed quickly and tossed the torn and dirty t-shirt into the trash barrel. Leonard was not the type to tell a lie, but he knew in that moment that if his mother asked where the t-shirt was, he'd say he'd lost it, because he couldn't bear to have to explain to his parents what had really happened. He decided he'd much rather endure a lecture on keeping track of one's belongings than to admit that he'd been humiliated by the other boys.

He had been so hopeful that the 1971-1972 academic year would be the year he was finally able to just blend in. He didn't care if the other kids liked him, he just didn't want to be bullied anymore. His head was pounding and he needed time to think, so he headed down to the nurse's office. The white-haired nurse led him to a cot, handed him an ice pack, and told him to "have a lie down" while she called his mother. While he was stretched out on the cot, with the ice pack on his forehead, he pondered what kind of affliction he might be able to acquire to avoid gym class for the rest of the year.

Chapter 23

Friday, September 7, 2018

Leonard was at his desk, preparing the monthly payroll reports, when he heard a familiar "click clack, click clack" sound of high heels coming down the hallway, followed by a knock on his office door.

"Knock knock!" Said Mary Beth, in her cheerful, sing-song voice, as she poked her head in. "There's cake in the break room... Stuart's turning the Big Four-Oh!"

"Oh," said Leonard "Thanks, Mary Beth."

He looked at the time on the corner of his computer screen: 11:53. He spent a few minutes finishing up what he'd been working on when Mary Beth arrived, then he opened his bottom left desk drawer to retrieve his Cup O'Noodles. Closing his office door behind him, he headed down the hall to the break room.

Because of the cake, it was more crowded than usual in the break room that day. Even people who usually went out for lunch came down to the break room when there was cake. As Leonard was heating the water for his soup in the microwave, he glanced over to the sheet cake sitting on the counter. It was a yellow cake with waxy-looking frosting, purchased from the discount supermarket. The lettering, which said, "Happy Birthd Stua" now that several slices were gone, was blue and gelatinous. He thought of Margaret, then, and hoped her she was enjoying her retirement. Because baking is her favorite hobby, she used to bring in homemade cakes for all the office celebrations. Margaret's cakes always reminded him of the cakes his dear mother, God rest her soul, used to bake.

"Hey Leonard! What are you smiling about, over there?"

Leonard looked up to see the guys from Shipping and Receiving all laughing in his general direction. Leonard felt his face flush with embarrassment. He wasn't sure what was so funny.

"Nothing," said Leonard, as he poured the hot water into his Cup O'Noodles, and headed over to his usual table.

Much to his relief, the guys didn't press the issue, and instead moved on to discussing something about some "big game" that was happening soon. Mike said something about "The Pats defense," which he pronounced, "Dee-Fence." Jim kept talking about a goat. Kevin referred to one of the players as a slang word for a woman's genitalia, which Leonard found to be quite inappropriate language for a work environment, as well as being tremendously disrespectful to women. Leonard had recently read an article in the newspaper about the rise of "Toxic Masculinity." He imagined that if that phrase were on the page of a dictionary, the accompanying photo would be of Mike, Jim and Kevin.

Chapter 24

September 9, 1971

When Leonard arrived at school for his second day of seventh grade, he did his best to blend into the crowd filing into the school building. As they all shuffled up the steps to the door, he overheard the conversation between two girls who were walking in front of him. One of the girls, said something about "Band, fourth period," and suddenly, Leonard knew exactly what to do to solve his gym class problem.

He broke away from the mass of schoolchildren heading to their home rooms, and marched directly to the guidance counselors office.

"Um, excuse me, Mr. Brown? Can I... um.... I have a question?"

"Certainly..." said the Guidance Counselor, sizing up the frail-looking boy before him. "You're Lawrence, right?"

"No, sir. I'm Leonard. Leonard Thompson."

"Leonard. Sorry. Well, what can I do for you, Leonard?"

"Um, I need to change my schedule."

Mr. Brown shuffled through some folders in the file cabinet next to his desk. "Oh, OK... is there a problem...?"

Leonard swallowed. "Um, it's just, I... well, I want to join the band?"

"Oh!" Replied Mr. Brown, who had finally located Leonard's file. "Band! What do you play?"

Leonard was starting to sweat. "Well, I...well, I was hoping... I want to learn something? Um, like... clarinet? Or..." He searched his panicked mind for the name of another instrument. "Or tuba?"

Mr. Brown pulled a paper out of the file and examined it. "OK, well, let's see. Hmm. We have one small issue. It seems the only free period you have is study hall, sixth period, and the band meets fourth period... and you have gym fourth period... "

Leonard cleared his throat, and tried to look as if he was just now coming up with this idea. "Oh, well, um... maybe I could move to a different gym class?"

So that was how Leonard started playing in his junior high school band. Mr Feeney, the band director, offered him the tuba first, but that didn't go so well. It was so large that Leonard could hardly lift it. And when he tried to play it, things only got worse. His cheeks puffed out, and he turned red and purple, and the only sound he managed to get out of it sounded more like a whoopie cushion than a tuba. Next he was given the flute, but after a week of that, Mr. Feeney suggested that perhaps the cymbals would be a better fit.

Leonard's junior high school years got a little better from there. The kids in band were nice to him, and although he discovered that he wasn't particularly musical, he did enjoy the experience. He was still harassed in the hallways between classes from time to time, and before and after school, but at least he didn't have any classes with Johnny Allen and his crew. He managed to avoid the social nightmare of the school cafeteria by gaining the favor of the school librarian, Mrs. Brady, who allowed him to eat his bagged lunch at the table by her desk, before giving him a stack of books that needed to be re-shelved. This turned out to be his favorite part of the school day. Mrs. Brady, was a kind, soft-spoken woman, with fluffy white hair and wire rimmed glasses that she wore attached to a chain around her neck. Since the other kids were all having lunch in the cafeteria, Leonard felt safe there in the library. It was just him, Mrs. Brady, and all those books. Sometimes they would talk about what he'd been reading, or what new books the library had acquired, but mostly they just enjoyed the quiet together.

Leonard continued to get excellent grades, and because he was quiet and respectful, and always did his homework, he was well-liked by all of his teachers. His report cards always noted what a pleasure he was to have in class, which, for Florence and Earl, was an even bigger point of pride than the A's he earned.

Chapter 25

Saturday, September 8, 2018

As Leonard was heading out to run his Saturday errands, he saw his neighbor, Patty. She was watering the pots of flowers she kept on her side of the stoop. As he locked the door and turned to head down the steps, she set down her watering can and looked at her watch. "Yup! Right on time..." she said, shaking her head.

Patty leaned on the railing between the two sides of their stoop, and squinted at Leonard. "You are really stuck in a rut, Leonard."

Leonard shrugged. He wasn't really sure what to say to that.

Patty continued. "I have lived here for five years, now, and that whole time, you've been coming and going at exactly the same times each day, week in, week out, winter, spring, summer and fall. Don't you get bored doing the same things all the time?"

Leonard blinked. "Um, no? I don't think so."

"You," Patty pointed at Leonard. "need to get a little excitement into your life. Spice things up a little bit."

But Leonard is not particularly fond of spicy things. He is well aware that his life would not be described as exciting. Some people, like Patty, for example, might even call it "boring." But Leonard doesn't really see that as a problem. He likes knowing what he's going to be doing each day, and he enjoys spending his evenings relaxing with a good book. Excitement, in Leonard's opinion, is really overrated. His life, these days, is safe and predictable, which is exactly how he likes it.

Chapter 26

1976

Throughout his childhood, Leonard's parents often worried that their son didn't really have friends. They'd noticed that the other children in their neighborhood would be out playing ball in the street, or riding around on their bikes, but Leonard never joined them. Instead, he preferred to climb up into the apple tree in their backyard with a book, or build model planes in his room, or peruse the Funke and Wagnell's Encyclopedia set that Earl kept on the bookcase in their living room.

But things began to work themselves out by high school. Leonard joined the math team, and became good friends with two of his teammates, Paul and Kenneth. The boys would study together, and would quiz each other on the bus on the way to math team meets. Leonard enjoyed hanging out with Paul and Kenneth, playing board games down in Paul's family's rumpus room, trading books and comics, or going to the movies. But Leonard was always an introvert at heart; it was never a huge priority for him to have a large group of friends. Even as a teenager, he was the type who preferred a quiet evening by the fire with a good book over a big, noisy party.

During their senior year of high school, Leonard's friends both chose universities out of state— Kenneth was accepted at Yale, and Paul at Oberlin— but Leonard decided to attend the local state college instead. His high school guidance counselor had questioned this decision.

"You're an excellent student, Leonard." He told him. "You have the grades to get into a good private college. Honestly, I think you could get into Harvard if you want to."

Leonard sat quietly, looking at his hands folded in his lap as Mr. Bryant argued his case for an Ivy League education. When it seemed like he was finished. Leonard looked up at him across the desk.

"Yes, sir... thank you... but, I want to go to college here."

For Leonard, the choice seemed obvious. He had a college fund that his parents had set up for him when he was born, which would likely be almost enough to pay his way through the state college, especially if he lived at home and commuted, which is exactly what he planned to do...partly for the cost, but mostly because he couldn't imagine living in the dorms. That felt far too scary and unpredictable for someone who'd suffered so much bullying from his peers. In order to pay for a private college, he'd need more money from his parents, (which he would not dream of asking them for) as well as taking out loans, and that just didn't seem sensible. He felt he could get a fine education at the state college, without going into debt. Besides, his Dad had gone to the same state college, and Leonard knew it would it make him very proud if his son would also be a student there.

And so, in spite of Mr. Bryant's protests, that's exactly what Leonard did. He applied, and was readily accepted, and because of his excellent academic record, he received some very generous scholarships. He lived at home with his parents, as he always had, and commuted to school each day for his classes.

Leonard very much enjoyed his experience with higher education. At college there were no bullies to distract him from his studies. How wonderful it was to be able to go to classes every day and never once have to hear someone shout, "Leonard the Lion!" And he didn't have to take gym at college, either, thank goodness. He also enjoyed getting to stretch his wings academically, learning about things he'd never really thought much about in high school, like Art History, Astronomy, and World Religions. He loved the college library, which was much larger than his town library. He spent many long hours there, reading, studying and doing homework, surrounded by more books than he'd ever seen in one place.

Leonard wrapped up his first semester with a 4.0, and Florence baked him his favorite carrot cake, with her famous cream cheese frosting, to celebrate. As they sat together at the kitchen table, enjoying the cake, Earl said, "Now son, we are so proud of how hard you're working at school. Good grades are important. But, college is a special time in your life. Try to have a little fun, too."

The next semester, Leonard joined the Chess Club.

Chapter 27

Saturday, September 8, 2018

Leonard was in the soup aisle, perusing the cans of Campbell's Soup.

"Leonard?"

Leonard nearly jumped out of his skin, as he had never, to his recollection, had someone call him by name at the grocery store. He turned toward the voice, his panic slowly turning to recognition.

"Kenneth! What a surprise!"

Kenneth laughed, extending his hand. "Sorry, I didn't mean to scare you. How are you, man? It's been ages!" They shook hands, and Kenneth clapped Leonard on the shoulder with his other hand.

"I'm good! Are you in town for a visit?"

Kenneth shook his head. "I wish. I'm here to sell my parent's house. They're going to stay in Florida full time. It's too much for them to go back and forth now. And, my sister is living down there now, so she'll be nearby. "

"Oh, that's nice." Said Leonard. "How are your parents doing?"

"Well, My dad had a stroke a couple of months ago."

"Oh, I'm so sorry to hear that."

"Thanks," Kenneth shrugged. "He's doing alright. Getting some mobility back, with the physical therapy."

"Well, that's good." Said Leonard. "And how is your mom?"

"Stubborn as ever." Kenneth laughed. "Eighty-seven years old, and still insists on doing everything herself. Last week my sister caught her standing on the coffee table, trying to dust the ceiling fan."

"Oh my!" Said Leonard.

"Hey, have you seen Paul lately?" Kenneth asked.

Leonard cleared his throat. "No, I haven't. It's been quite a while, actually. I'm embarrassed to say that the last time I saw him was at his mother's funeral. I think that was about two years ago now, wasn't it?"

Kenneth nodded. "Sounds about right."

"How's Lisa?" Leonard asked.

"She's good! She's been busy, helping our youngest, Ashley, plan her wedding,"

"Wow," said Leonard. "Ashley's getting married! Time flies, doesn't it?"

"Sure does." Said Kenneth. "They're doing a 'destination wedding.' That's a thing now, apparently." He rolled his eyes.

Leonard wasn't entirely sure what a "destination wedding" was, but since Kenneth was now looking at his watch, Leonard decided not to ask.

"I better get going. I have a meeting with the Realtor. Hey, let's not wait for the next funeral to get together, huh?"

Leonard nodded.

Kenneth smiled. "It was so good to see you."

"You too." Said Leonard, waving as Kenneth headed down

the aisle.

Leonard thought about their high school days, when his friendship with Kenneth and Paul was easy and comfortable. As teenagers, none of them would have imagined a time when they wouldn't see each other nearly every day. After the three of them had all gone to different colleges, they still managed to hang out together on holiday breaks. But soon, Kenneth moved away, then Paul got married, and they all had busy careers, and adult responsibilities. Soon their friendship was just a yearly Christmas card, and the occasional funeral, where they'd promise to get together more often.

Leonard regrets not making more of an effort to keep those promises.

He turned his attention back to the soup, and placed seven cans in his cart.

Chapter 28

1980

After he graduated with his degree in Accounting, it was time for Leonard to find himself a job. He prepared his resume, typed up on official-looking creamy linen paper, as his college advisor had recommended, and began applying for some bookkeeping and accounting jobs. A few weeks after he'd begun his job search, Meyer & Son Manufacturing was the first to call him in for an interview.

He was very nervous about the whole thing, and he felt his underarms growing damp as he sat across from Mr. Meyer, doing his best to appear composed and competent. As Leonard was walking back to the bus stop after the interview was over, he was sure he'd blown it by saying all the wrong things. But much to his surprise, Mr. Meyer's secretary called the following week and offered Leonard the job. He was relieved that he'd been hired. It seemed like a good company to work for, and it was just a short bus ride away from home, in the next town over, so he wouldn't have too long of a commute. But mostly, he was relieved that, for the time being, he would not have to go out on any more job interviews, since the very idea made him break out in hives.

His parents were so proud that he'd gotten a job so quickly, especially in such difficult economic times, but, of course, they were not surprised. Their son, their Miracle Child, was very smart and capable, and had been given wonderful letters of recommendation from his college professors. Earl was especially proud that his son had followed in his footsteps, and chose to go into accounting.

As he thought about embarking on this new chapter, he felt, for the first time in his life, really, thrilled at the idea of being a grown up. He was also really looking forward to earning his first real paycheck. Now that he was a twenty-two-year-old adult, working a full-time job, he felt it was time that he contribute to the household expenses. He brought this up to his parents over dinner.

"Oh, Leonard!" Florence exclaimed, shaking her head. "I simply cannot bear the thought of you paying rent to live in our family home! My goodness! You're our *son*..." She pinched his cheek. "It just doesn't seem right."

"Momma," said Leonard. "I am an adult with a full-time job. It doesn't seem right that I should live here rent free. I'll always be your son, but I'm not a child anymore. I want to contribute. I want to pull my own weight."

"Nonsense." Florence said, crossing her arms over her ample bosom. "You pull your weight just fine, by helping Dad with the lawn, and taking out the trash, and being a good son to us."

After much discussion, a compromise was made. She and Earl finally agreed to accept a small sum from Leonard each month, to help with a portion of the utility and grocery bills. Earl, who'd recently retired after forty years as a Certified Public Accountant, had always done his best to instill in his son the importance of responsible money management, so he suggested that Leonard put the rest of the amount he'd planned to give them into a savings account, to save for his future.

"It's always a good idea to have a nest egg," Earl told him.

"Indeed," replied Florence. "A penny saved, is a penny earned."

Chapter 29

Tuesday, September 18, 2018

On Tuesday, September 18, 2018, instead of the ringing bell sound he was accustomed to, Leonard was awakened by the sound of a whimpering dog through his open bedroom window. He looked at his alarm clock on the bedside table: 2:47. There was sunshine streaming in the window, so Leonard realized that couldn't be right... it was far too bright outside for 2:47am. He hauled himself out of bed and went downstairs to check the kitchen clock. 7:48! Panicked, he did his best to pull himself together and get dressed as quickly as possible, under these highly unusual circumstances. He grabbed his briefcase and rushed out the door, without having his oatmeal, stepping on the newspaper and nearly tripping on the strange dog that was sitting on his stoop. He did not have time to stop and wonder *why* there was a dog on his stoop. He ran toward the bus stop, but he was still a full block away as he saw the bus pull away from the bus stop, out onto the road and drive away.

"Wait!" Leonard called, waving his briefcase.

He didn't get too far before his hastily tied shoes got the better of him, and he found himself face down on the sidewalk. His heart was thumping so loudly in his ears that it took him a moment to realize that someone was talking to him. He sat up, and fought to open his eyes against the glare of the sun. His glasses were dangling from one ear, the lenses resting between his nose and upper lip. He pushed them up to their proper location, and blinked at the woman's face peering down at him, the morning sun surrounding her head like a halo. Leonard wondered if maybe he had actually died.

"ARE YOU OK??" The Angel asked him. "Should I call 911?"

The Angel sounded a bit familiar. Blinking and squinting to see through the sun's glare, he realized that it was not an angel, after all. It was Patty, out walking her dog, Barney. For a split second, Leonard felt relieved to find that he was still among the living. But as his head began to clear and the reality of his situation became evident, he was suddenly overcome with embarrassment. He was mortified, really. He grabbed for his briefcase and scrambled to his feet. It occurred to Leonard at that moment while he'd survived falling on the pavement, it was now entirely possible that he might die of humiliation.

"Sorry, um... I just... no need, it's..." And, not knowing what else to do, he turned around and hurried back toward home.

Patty had been alarmed to find Leonard on the ground, and she wondered for a moment if she should follow him. But she decided to just let him go, figuring if he was able to hurry off like that, he must not be injured too badly. That Leonard certainly is an odd duck.

Leonard arrived back at the condo to find the strange dog still there on the stoop. It just sat there on the mat in front of his door, right next to the newspaper. He stopped at the bottom step and stared up at the medium-sized mutt, which looked (and smelled) like it could use a bath, and a good brushing. In return, the dog perked up its scruffy ears, and wagged its tail hopefully. Just then, Leonard heard the sound of the phone ringing through the open window. It was a proper phone, plugged into the wall, which is how Leonard liked it. Although Patty had told him, on more than one occasion, "No one has a landline these days, Leonard." He stepped over the dog, unlocked the door, and hurried inside. He dropped his briefcase by the door, and answered the phone on the fourth ring.

"Leonard!" It was his boss, Mr. Meyer, the son of his former boss, Mr. Meyer, who had long since retired. "It's 8:37! Dolores was worried, because you're never late. What's going on? You sick or something?"

"Um, not exactly?" replied Leonard.

"Well, Leonard... you haven't taken a day off in years..."

"Twenty-four years, in fact." said Leonard, as he looked down at the gravel embedded in his palm.

"Listen, Mary Beth over in HR says she's been trying to get you to take some of the PTO you have built up, and you sound like you could use a little break. We'll see you next week!"

Panic rose in Leonard's chest, and he tried to protest, but Mr. Meyer had already hung up.

Leonard swallowed hard, and hung up the phone. He was distraught.

Chapter 30

1980

After Leonard accepted the job at Meyer & Son Manufacturing, Florence had gone to the back of her closet, to get the special gift she'd been saving for their son. It was an old brown leather briefcase. She asked Earl to take it down to Jerry, the cobbler in town who resoled Earl's wingtips, to have it spruced up a bit. Jerry did a fine job, reinforcing the stitching, and polishing the old leather until it looked almost like new.

The evening before Leonard's first day at Meyer & Son, as they were finishing up dinner, Earl leaned back in his chair.

"Leonard, I left a box over by the front door... mind getting that for me?"

"Sure, Dad...." Said Leonard, as he stood up and headed out to the living room. He came back into the kitchen carrying a brown box, and set it down on the table in front of his father.

"Go ahead and open it, son."

Leonard noticed that his father had winked at his mother, and wondered what was going on. He carefully removed the top of the box, to find layers of tissue paper. Earl nodded at him to continue, so he reached in, and unwrapped a chestnut–

brown leather briefcase. Up near the handle was embossed, LJT, Leonard's initials.

"For me?" He said, a little overwhelmed.

Florence nodded. "For you, Sweetheart. It belonged to my father. But we had your initials added, to make it your own."

"This was Leonard's?" He said quietly, almost to himself, as he turned the case around, examining it. "My Grandfather?" He opened it, and saw a small label sewn inside: *Dr. Leonard Anderson, MD.*

"Do you like it, Sweetheart?" Florence asked. "I wasn't sure, if maybe you'd prefer to have a new one."

"This is perfect." Leonard said. "I love it. Thank you." Although he never knew his grandfather, he felt a tremendous amount of admiration for him, based on the stories he'd been told, by his mother and Aunt Eleanor. He felt honored to have been given this wonderful gift.

"I'm so glad, Dear." Said Florence. "Your grandfather would be so proud to have such a bright and accomplished grandson."

With the money he had saved from the part-time job he had at the local market while he was a student, Leonard bought himself some smart new work clothes from JC Penney: four pairs of dress slacks, five cotton dress shirts, three ties, and a new pair of dress shoes. Leonard prepared carefully for his first day at his new job, because he really wanted to make a good impression. His mother had ironed all of his new shirts for him, and had ironed his new slacks with sharp creases. He polished his shoes to a perfect shine, and was very careful in tying his new tie into a tidy knot. He'd chosen a simple blue and black striped tie, because that seemed to be the one that looked most professional, in Leonard's opinion. With his new briefcase packed, he headed out the door, stopping to wave back to his mother, who was watching him though the big picture window, beaming with pride, waving and blowing him kisses.

When he arrived at Meyer & Son Manufacturing that first day, a nice lady named Pam showed him around the place. The front of the brick building was where all the company's offices were located: Customer service, bookkeeping, personnel, etc, while the factory, and shipping and receiving, were located at the back of the building. The executive suite (where Leonard had been interviewed) was on the second floor. After Pam had pointed out the break room, smoking area, and restrooms, she introduced him to his supervisor, Frank, a fellow who reminded Leonard of the character Lou Grant from *The Mary Tyler Moore Show*. Frank showed Leonard to his desk, in the office shared by the three employees of the bookkeeping department, and went over the responsibilities of the job.

Later that day, Leonard was sitting at his desk, reconciling the stack of receipts he'd be given to sort out by his supervisor, when he heard someone singing "Freebird" out in the hallway. Leonard, quite surprised and confused, looked toward the open door of their office, and saw a teenage boy on a skateboard whiz past the doorway and down the hallway, still singing.

"What was that all about?" Leonard asked Joe, who occupied the desk across from him.

"Oh, that's Mr. Meyer's son, Chip." Said Joe, rolling his eyes.

"He looks young. Shouldn't he be in school?" Asked Leonard.

"Yeah, he's 15. Probably came by to ask his Daddy for money." Replied Joe. "He's a royal pain-in-the-ass, and a complete fuck up. But his dad is the boss, so we all just have to pretend he's not. It's maddening."

At the time of this conversation, Leonard had no idea that some twenty years later, when Mr. Meyer retired at the age of seventy, the pain-in-the-ass fuck up would become his new boss.

Chapter 31

September 18, 2018

Leonard paced up and down the hallway, nervously wringing his hands, replaying the telephone conversation with Mr. Meyer in his head. He tried to figure out what the heck had just happened. Mr. Meyer had a most infuriating habit of getting his way by talking fast and not letting the other person get a word in. Then, he'd abruptly end the conversation and be gone, leaving no opportunity for a response. This was one of the many reasons Leonard had preferred working for the first Mr. Meyer. He was a much more reasonable person than his son.

Leonard realized he was sweating profusely. He went into the bathroom and splashed cold water on his face. His head was spinning, and he could not gather his thoughts. He needed to calm himself down, so he could think things through, and figure out what to do. He sat on the edge of the tub, took some deep breaths, and tried to will his heart rate to slow down. He needed to make some sort of a plan, because he had no idea what to do if he couldn't go to work. It was a Tuesday, for God's sake!

As he sat there taking calming breathes, Leonard suddenly

remembered there was a dog on his stoop. This sent his mind spinning in a completely different direction. Why the heck was there a dog on his stoop? Leonard stood up, went out to the front door and opened it. Sure enough, the dog was still there, sitting on the doormat as if it belonged there.

"Go home." Leonard told the dog.

The dog didn't move. It just looked up at Leonard and wagged its tail. Leonard sighed, stepped past the dog, and sat on the top step, his head in his hands. He was completely overwhelmed by the morning's events. The dog turned itself around, and sat down right next to him.

"Leonard! You got a dog!"

It was Patty, returning from her walk with Barney, who nodded a hello at the other dog.

"I didn't," said Leonard, not looking up, his head still in his hands.

Patty looked back and forth between Leonard and the dog. Then she squinted at Leonard, her hands on her hips. "What the heck is going on with you today, Leonard?"

"It's a long story," he replied.

"Well. Good thing I've got coffee on..." said Patty.

Chapter 32

December 1983

During the holiday season, Leonard had visited with his old high school friends. It had been a while, and it was good to see them again. Kenneth had completed his Masters, and was living in Connecticut, working at his Alma mater, Yale. Paul had moved back home to his parents' house after graduating from Oberlin, but had recently moved into an apartment with his fiancee. This got Leonard to thinking that it was probably about time for him to move out of his parents house, as well.

He had been working at Meyer & Son for a little over three years, and because he had followed his father's advice, he had built up a pretty good nest egg. He had begun to peruse the real estate section of the newspaper regularly, but so far, he hadn't seen anything that fit what he had in mind. He was hoping to find himself a nice little condo, or a small house, that wouldn't be too far from his job or from his parents. He was hoping for something that didn't need any major renovations, and wouldn't require too much in the way of maintenance. And of course, it needed to fit his budget.

That spring, on his way home from work one Friday evening,

Leonard noticed a "For Sale" sign in front of a condo that was just a few blocks from the bus stop, about a half mile away from his parents house. The location was pretty much perfect: right near the center of town, close to the library, the post office, a cafe and a corner store. It was also comfortably within his price range. Earl helped his son find a mortgage with a suitable interest rate, and with his nest egg for a down payment, Leonard became a homeowner.

Florence was proud that Leonard had grown into such a responsible and capable man, and it brought her so much joy to see her child so happy. Leonard's happiness meant everything to her! But she had also been dreading the day her Miracle Child would fly from the nest. She always knew it would happen, of course. A mother raises her child with the expectation that they will become a self-sufficient adult someday. But to have that moment be imminent was almost more than Florence could bear. She kept up a brave face for weeks, but on his last night at home, she could not stop crying.

"Oh, Momma..." Leonard told her, "It's not like you're never going to see me again... I'm only going to be a half mile away!"

This made Florence cry harder.

Though Leonard did not ever admit this to his mother, he also cried, that last night at home. As he lay on his childhood bed, in his childhood bedroom, the moonlight through the trees casting shadows on his wall, he was overcome by emotion. He'd been surprised by those tears. He was a grown man, and was excited to have a home of his own. He had not expected that there would also be a deep sadness in the knowledge that it was the last night he'd be living under their roof. And tomorrow morning would be the last morning he'd wake to the smell of coffee brewing in the old percolator, and the sound of his mother humming quietly as she puttered around the kitchen, fixing breakfast.

After he moved out, he called his mother several times a week, and he went back home to visit his parents every Sunday afternoon. They would all have lunch together... grilled cheese sandwiches and tomato soup... and then Leonard would help his father with the tasks around the house that were getting difficult for them, now that they were getting on in years.

Chapter 33

September 18, 2018

"Have a seat," said Patty, gesturing to the small, round, kitchen table, which was covered with a colorful vintage tablecloth. Each of the four chairs at the table were painted a different color. Leonard sat in the orange chair, as that was the one closest to him. He sat quietly and looked around the bright, sunny room. There were houseplants hanging in the windows, and photos of smiling people stuck to the refrigerator with assorted magnets. Patty got two mugs out of the cabinet, and poured the coffee.

Leonard had never been inside Patty's side of the duplex before, and she'd never been in his. This suddenly seemed strange to him, as they had lived next door to each other for five years now, and talked to each other several times a week.

"Cream? Sugar?" Asked Patty, setting the mugs on the table.

"No, thank you." Said Leonard.

He looked down at the mug Patty had placed in front of him, turning it slightly to read the words that were printed on it. The mug was pink, with lettering meant to look like it was written in crayon. It said, "When Mom says NO, just ask AUNTIE."

Patty noticed him examining the mug, and chuckled.

"Yeah, I know it's silly. It was a gift from my niece." She poured creamer into her mug, and sat down across from Leonard.

"OK." She squinted at him again. "Don't take this the wrong way, Leonard... but you look a wreck. What's wrong?"

He sipped his coffee, then took a deep breath. "Well... I... I'm not sure where to begin..."

He looked up at Patty, who nodded encouragingly.

"Well," Leonard cleared his throat. "My mother, God rest her soul, gave me an alarm clock for my college graduation..."

"OK..." said Patty, not entirely sure where this was going. "An alarm clock? That's an unusual graduation gift."

"Yes, I suppose it is." Leonard replied, as if only just now considering that this could be the case. "It's because of the quote... from Ben Franklin. 'You will find the key to success under the alarm clock.' She was very fond of useful sayings." He paused, thinking about this, then cleared his throat again. "So... well, you see, I've relied on that clock to wake me up every morning at 6:30am, for the last thirty-seven years. But today, it didn't...and, well.... I woke up, but the alarm hadn't gone off... and the clock said 2:47, but it was actually 7:48, and my bus is at 8:07." He heaved a sigh.

"Well, my goodness," said Patty. "Thirty seven years of usefulness for an alarm clock is pretty good, I think... isn't it?"

"But, you see... I'm never, ever late..." Leonard looked like he might cry. He took another deep breath. "And, well, tried to get to the bus stop, but I tripped."

"Yes, sir, you sure did. You really had me worried there, for a minute. I thought you'd passed out or something."

Leonard shook his head, and looked down at his coffee cup. "Ugh...it's just... so embarrassing..."

"Leonard, please. I'm a nurse. I have seen things you would not believe. Tripping on the sidewalk is definitely not a reason to be embarrassed. It's not like I found you with a can of hairspray in your rectum."

Leonard swallowed, eyes wide. "Really?!" He practically whispered. "That's happened?!"

Patty laughed. "Things you would not believe, Leonard. Anyway... continue with your story..."

Leonard shook his head, to clear the unfortunate image that information conjured in his mind. "Um, well, I got back home, and, and my boss called..." He paused.

"Go on... was he upset, because you were late?" Patty asked.

"Uh, No... actually. Um, he told me to get some rest. And said he'd see me in a week." Leonard's brow was furrowed.

Patty was really doing her best to understand all of this.

"Oh. But that's good? Right? That was nice of him?"

Leonard shook his head. "That's when I really panicked..."

"What? Wait...You... I don't understand... Why?"

Again, Leonard looked like he might cry. "I haven't missed a day of work in twenty-four years."

"That's.... Really?? You haven't missed a single day of work in twenty-four years?"

He shook his head. "Well except weekends and holidays... but other than that, no... not since..." He looked down at the table, his voice quiet again. "Not since my mother's funeral."

"Oh..." Said Patty, softening.

They sat there a moment, in silence, Leonard staring at his cup, Patty staring at Leonard.

Patty leaned forward "Well, then," she said, gently. "It's about time you did, Leonard. Don't you think?"

"But I... I just can't. I wouldn't even know what to do."

Patty smiled, and sat back in her chair. "Well I've got news for you, Leonard. You're doing it right now, and you're just fine. It's 9:45 am on a Tuesday, and you're having coffee with a friend instead of working. And you're still alive. Aren't you?"

Leonard looked surprised. "Yes, " he said, his shoulders relaxing. "I suppose I am."

Patty got up to pour more coffee, and placed a box of Entenmann's coffee cake and two plates on the table.

"I have one more question for you, Leonard." She pointed to the strange dog, who was lying on the floor next to Barney. "Whose dog is that?"

Leonard, who, with everything else going on, had very nearly forgotten about it, looked down at the dog, then back to Patty.

"I have no idea."

Chapter 34

March 1989

Earl collapsed while going out to get the paper one morning. He had walked down the front steps, bent to pick up the paper from the flagstone walkway, and when he stood up again to head back to the house, Florence saw his face contort into a grimace as his body crumpled onto the ground. Their next door neighbor, Evelyn, heard Florence cry out, and called for an ambulance. Earl was rushed to the hospital, but it was too late. He had died of a massive heart attack, at the age of seventy-six. He had heart issues for years, but still, his passing was unexpected. He had been on medications for his blood pressure, and Florence had to keep an eye on his cholesterol, but other than that he seemed just fine. He stayed active; he was in a bowling league, and he and Florence walked to church together every Sunday morning. It just seemed impossible that he was really gone.

Of course, Leonard was terribly worried about how his dear mother would manage on her own, without his father. After the funeral was over, Leonard offered to fix up the spare bedroom in his condo for her, so she wouldn't have to be all alone in the house, but she just couldn't bear the thought of leaving the home she'd shared with her beloved, Earl.

"Oh, Leonard. I just can't leave this house." They were sitting at the kitchen table, where they'd shared thousands of meals together as a family. "I spent forty-six years here with your father. And in this house, I was blessed with my Miracle Child," She reached out to take his hand in hers. "I raised you in this house, Leonard. I have too many memories here. I can't leave."

Leonard understood, but still, he worried about her. "I just want to make sure you'll be OK, Momma. Will you manage alright here, by yourself, without Dad?"

"I'll be OK, Sweetheart. I have Evelyn and Stan right next door, and you're only a few minutes away. This is my home, and it's where I belong."

Leonard nodded. Imagining his mother without his father was like imagining a left shoe without the right. They were a pair. Momma and Dad. "Are you sure?" He asked.

"Your father was the love of my life, Leonard. I miss him terribly, and I know that I always will. You never really stop missing the ones you love after they're gone."

Leonard wiped a tear from his cheek. "Never?"

"Well, it does get easier to bear, over time, but it never goes away completely. Some losses are easier to accept than others. Grandma Alice nearly saw her hundredth birthday! I miss her, but she lived a full life, and it was her time." She winked at Leonard then, an acknowledgment that Grandma Alice was, as they say, "a piece of work."

"But," Florence continued, "some losses feel impossible to bear. When Jimmy was taken from us so young, and then, Aunt Eleanor..."

Florence always choked up when talking about her younger sister, who'd died ten years earlier, at the age of sixty-two, just a year after finding a lump in her breast.

She collected herself, and went on. "I have never even imagined a life without my Earl. I don't know how I'm going to do this. I will miss him every single day, for the rest of my time here. Because that's the price we pay for love. But, I promise you, Sweetheart, it's worth it. Because love is everything in this life."

Leonard nodded, too choked up to speak.

"We were so lucky to have your father. He was ours, and we were his, and he loved us. And we loved him. I'm so, so grateful for that." Florence took her son's hand. "And I believe he is still with us, Leonard! Watching over us. And I know we'll see him again someday."

Leonard was glad his mother had her faith to comfort her, as she coped with this devastating loss. But for Leonard, who'd stopped going to church by the time he started college, the idea of loved ones in "heaven" just sounded like a tall tale; try as he might, he couldn't quite convince himself of the existence of a hereafter. For him, there was no hope of a reunion at the Pearly Gates. For him, there was just a void where he once had a father.

As Leonard was heading home, promised he'd call her every evening after work to check on her, and of course he'd be there every Sunday, as usual, to help her with things around the house.

"You're such a good son, Leonard. You've been such a Blessing to me."

Florence found her grief to be a complicated beast. She just missed Earl so very much. She missed the way he would tell her about interesting stories in the newspaper as she cooked breakfast. She missed the bouquets of flowers he brought her every Friday. She missed watching Jeopardy with him in the evenings. She managed alright during the day, when she could keep herself busy. But the nights— when everything was quiet, and she was all alone in the house— were sometimes almost unbearable. She'd taken to sitting in Earl's recliner to watch television, instead of her rocking chair, because it made her feel closer to him.

One evening, soon after Earl's passing, Florence settled into his recliner with a cup of Salada tea and her knitting, to watch Jeopardy. She read the tea bag tag aloud.

"Tea time is a moment to pause and reflect."

As the show's familiar theme song began to play, Florence had a sudden realization. It occurred to her that, up until Earl's death, she had never, ever lived alone. She'd gone from living with her parents, to living with Earl. For the past forty-six years, her life had primarily revolved around her husband, and later, also her son. She had truly loved being a wife and mother, more than anything else she'd ever done. But it didn't take too long before she began to find a sort of freedom in living alone. She liked that she didn't have to cook dinner if she didn't feel like it, and she liked that there was less laundry, and that she could come and go as she pleased, without having to worry she'd be inconveniencing anyone. She felt terribly guilty about this for the longest time, until she realized that both things could exist together: She could still miss Earl tremendously, still feel his absence in every corner of their home, and also enjoy the life she had now. She knew that Earl would want that for her. For the rest of her life, she talked to Earl every night before she went to sleep, to tell him about her day.

Chapter 35

Tuesday, September 18, 2018

A funny thing happened there in Patty's kitchen that morning. Leonard realized that all of the things that seemed so bad and scary an hour ago felt much less so, now that he had spoken them out loud to Patty. It actually seemed almost silly, that he'd been so bent out of shape.

Patty knelt down next to the dog. "Who's your owner, sweet girl?"

"How do you know it's a girl?" Leonard asked.

"I'm a nurse, Leonard. I know."

Leonard blushed. "Right. Of course. Sorry."

"I'm sure someone's looking for her." Patty said, reaching for her iPhone. She snapped a photo of the dog, and began tapping away on the phone. "We'll find your people," she told the dog. "Let's get that pretty face on Nextdoor."

"On what?"

"Oh Leonard."

While Patty was posting the dog's photo to the local Nextdoor page, and to a local Lost Pet page on Facebook, she explained Nextdoor. As she finished the posts, she set her phone on the table, and looked at Leonard.

"Leonard Thompson. It is the year of our Lord, two thousand eighteen. Don't you think it's time you finally got a cell phone?"

Leonard just shrugged.

They finished up their coffee cake, then decided to see if anyone at the Dog Park might recognize the lost dog. Patty found one of Barney's old collars and an extra leash, and together they started walking.

"Have you ever had a dog?" Patty asked Leonard.

"No. My Dad had asthma, and was allergic to animals, so I wasn't allowed to have any pets growing up. Well, actually, I did have a goldfish, when I was about 6. I won it at a fair. But it only lived a few months."

"Oh no..." said Patty. "Fish can be like that..."

"Yeah. I came home from school one day and found it floating in its bowl. That was rough. Boy, did I cry. After my mom flushed it down the toilet, she cleaned out the fish bowl, added it to the box of donations for the church rummage sale, then instituted a strict "no more pets" policy" because she couldn't stand to see me so upset." He chuckled at the memory.

"It sounds like she was a wonderful mother."

"Oh, she was the best. I really miss her. Both of my parents were great. I think I had a pretty good home life as a child, compared to a lot of people."

"Well, that's not something you hear everyday," Said Patty with a chuckle.

"That's true," Leonard smiled. "I know I was very, very lucky."

"Did you ever want to get married? Have a family?"

Leonard nodded. "I always thought I would. When I was young, I imagined I'd get married and have a child, just same as my parents. But it just... didn't work out that way."

Patty looked at him thoughtfully. "Was it just, that you didn't meet the right girl?"

Leonard shrugged. "I almost got engaged once. Her name was Anne. We met at college. We'd been dating for almost a year, and things were going well. So I bought a ring, and went to her parent's house, and asked for their blessing. Her father patted me on the back and her mother cried. The next night, we went out to dinner. I had the ring in my pocket. But after the waiter took our orders, she said, 'We need to talk.'"

Patty gasped. "Oh no... "

Leonard smiled and shook his head. "Yeah. She said she wanted to see other people."

"Oh God... that is the worst. Did you tell her? That you were going to propose?"

Leonard shook his head. "Didn't see the point. After it was all over, and my bruised ego had a chance to recover, I realized we weren't really meant to be. I mean, we got along well. We never argued. I think maybe I confused that with love? But really, we didn't have much in common. So, after Anne, I think I was a little gun shy. I went out with a few other women, here and there, but nothing got serious. Over time, I just got occupied with work, and helping my parents. and I just got set in my ways."

Patty nodded. "I can see how that could happen. We all get stuck sometimes. I spent twenty years in a terrible marriage, because I kept thinking staying was easier than leaving."

"Wow," said Leonard. "Twenty years. That's a long time."

"It sure was. I should have left long before. I regret that I didn't. Sometimes I think about the life I could have had... maybe I'd have been able to have kids. I don't know..."

110

"Did you want to have kids? With Todd?" Leonard asked.

"When we were dating, we talked about having kids someday. I was twenty-seven at the time, about to start grad school, and it felt like I had all the time in the world. I was thirty when we got married, and I wanted to get established in my nursing career before starting a family. But the time just never felt right. Looking back, I think I just knew deep down that Todd wouldn't be a good father. And then, next thing I knew, I was in my forties, and I realized that window was closing."

Patty looked so sad, then. Leonard wanted to say something to comfort her, but he didn't know what to say.

Patty looked up at Leonard, and continued. "I looked into adoption after I left Todd. But, I was paying off the attorney fees from my divorce for more than two years, and well... I just figured, it wasn't meant to be."

"I'm sorry." Said Leonard.

"No, it's OK, really... I've made peace with it. I have my nephews and my niece, and they are my favorite people in the whole entire world. I love being an Auntie. All the fun of having kids, without the responsibility." She said with a smile. "And the thing is, now that I've been on my own for five years... I've learned that I don't really mind living alone. When I left Todd, my father and my sisters were so worried I'd be lonely. But the thing is, I was lonely while I lived with Todd, but not at all in the five years since I divorced him. I know, that sounds weird..."

Leonard shook his head. "No, it doesn't sound weird at all! I totally understand. I feel the same way. I've lived alone for such a long time, and, most of the time, I like it. I think it would be very hard for me to live with anyone else at this point in my life. And, yeah, I don't feel lonely at home, alone. The times I've felt the most lonely have almost always been when I was with other people."

Chapter 36

October 1994

Leonard was in the living room, having a cup of tea after dinner. For some reason, he would always remember that he had been reading *Ishmael*, by Daniel Quinn, when the phone rang that evening. He looked at the clock on his way to the phone. It was 7:05 on a Wednesday night; his mother was at Bingo, so he couldn't imagine who would be calling.

He picked up the phone.

"Hello?"

"Leonard! Thank goodness you're home!"

"Mrs. Morris? Is everything ok?"

"It's your mother... she's on her way to the hospital."

Leonard had known instantly that this was something serious, because every other time he called his mother's friend and next door neighbor "Mrs. Morris" she would say, "Oh, Leonard... Please call me Evelyn," which, by the way, he could never quite bring himself to do.

"How... What happened?" Leonard asked, balancing the phone handset on his shoulder as he started putting on his shoes.

"Father James and Kathy are driving her over there right now. She fell... at Bingo. We had just arrived, and sat at our usual table, when she got a strange look on her face. I asked if she was OK, and she said she didn't feel well. When she stood up, she fell to the floor."

"Oh no..." replied Leonard, putting on his jacket.

"You know how your mother is... she brushed it off, didn't want anyone making a fuss... but we all insisted she go straight to the hospital."

"Of course." He grabbed his wallet from the hall table. "I'm heading over there right now. Thanks for letting me know, Mrs. Morris."

At the hospital, it was determined that a "mini-stroke" had likely caused Florence's fall in the church basement. It was also determined that she did not suffer any fractures from the fall, which they said was very lucky indeed for a woman of her age.

"A stroke? No, that can't be..." said Florence, when they told her what the tests had shown. "When my mother had a stroke, she couldn't speak. But I can speak just fine. I'm sure it's nothing. I've just been overdoing it lately."

"Not all stroke patients experience aphasia," the doctor informed them. "It depends which area of the brain was affected. What you experienced was a 'mini stroke' or Transient Ischemic Attack. They don't tend to cause any permanent damage, but they are a warning sign, that you could be at risk for a more serious stroke. So, we will recommend some lifestyle changes."

Leonard wanted to stay with his mother, until they'd gotten her transferred to a room, where she'd stay for a day or two for observation. But Florence, who hated to be a bother, would not hear of it.

"Leonard. You have work in the morning! You go on home. I'll be fine."

"I'll just stay until they get you settled in a room, then I'll head out." He told her.

"Oh, sweetheart. You're such a worrier. Just like your father." She smiled at her son. "I'm in good hands here. You best get yourself home. 'Early to bed, early to rise, makes a man healthy, wealthy and wise.'"

There was no point in arguing with her, so Leonard kissed his mother's cheek, and promised he would call to check on her in the morning. On the way home, he remembered an incident from a few weeks ago, when he'd come by for his regular Sunday visit.

He'd arrived at the usual time, just after noon, and as he reached for the doorknob, he found the front door locked. In all the Sundays that he'd been coming back "home" for lunch with his mother, the door had never, ever been locked. His mother was expecting him, after all. He knocked, and when there was no answer, he took his keys from his pocket and opened the door.

"Mom? Momma??" He called, panic rising in his voice. Just then, his mother came shuffling into the room, looking a bit disheveled.

"Oh Leonard... I'm terribly sorry. I was a bit tired... I sat down for a minute when I came in from church, and must have fallen asleep."

He was relieved to see her, but his heart was still beating very fast. She was not the napping type, so he was still worried that something might be wrong. "It's OK Momma, I had my key... come sit" he said, guiding her to the sofa.

"Oh, now don't make a fuss. I'm fine." She patted his cheek.

"I have some sandwiches to make, now don't I?"

The rest of their afternoon together was uneventful. After lunch, Leonard mowed the yard, took out the trash and tightened up the leaky kitchen faucet. When he finished, they had some tea and worked together on her jigsaw puzzle.

After the stroke, Leonard looked back on that day and wondered if the two events were related. He wished that he'd paid closer attention, and promised himself he'd keep a closer eye on her.

When Leonard called her hospital room the next morning, she reported that she was feeling much better, and was looking forward to sleeping in her own bed. Later that evening, when Leonard returned home from work, there was a message on his answering machine.

"Hello, my Leonard, it's Momma. It's about 2:30 in the afternoon. I'm home now. Evelyn and Stan picked me up. I didn't want to bother you while you were at work. Well, anyway... I just wanted to let you know. I'll talk to you soon. Love you. Bye, now."

He picked up the phone, and dialed her number.

"Hello?"

"Momma..."

"Leonard! Hello, dear. How was work today?"

"Mom, I thought they wanted to keep you at the hospital for observation?"

"Well, I'm feeling so much better now. Those sweet nurses have actual sick people to take care of... they don't need to be wasting their time fussing over me."

Leonard sighed. That was so like his mother, not wanting to be a bother. "Well, then, can I bring you anything? Have you had dinner?"

"Oh, I'm good, Sweetheart. I had some leftovers in the fridge, so I heated those up. And Evelyn brought over a nice banana bread for me, so I can have that if I get a little peckish later. Don't you worry about me."

"Are you sure, Mom? I don't want you doing too much. You need to rest."

"Well, there is one thing I've been meaning to ask you to do. No rush, it can wait until you come on Sunday. Will you take the air conditioner out and put it in the attic? We're most certainly past the hot weather at this point."

"Of course I'll take care of that for you." said Leonard. "Maybe give the lawn a mowing, too, while I'm there."

"Oh, Leonard. You are such a Blessing to me."

As he hung up the phone that evening, he had no idea that this was to be the very last conversation he would ever have with his mother.

Chapter 37

Tuesday, September 18, 2018

No one at the park recognized the lost dog. Leonard and Patty took the dogs on a long walk around the neighborhood, to see if anyone had put up posters, but they didn't see anything. As they made their way back, Patty looked over at Leonard.

"You've got a little color back in your cheeks, Leonard! Are you feeling better?"

"I am, actually.... I feel much better. Thank you."

As they approached the duplex, Patty checked the time on her phone. "Oh! 12:15 already! Hey...Will you be alright keeping an eye on our scruffy little friend here on your own for a little while?"

"Yes, of course" said Leonard, though he suddenly realized he didn't know much about dogs. "Um, will she need anything? Like food, or...?" He had noticed his own stomach starting to growl. It was past lunchtime, after all.

Patty was filling two bowls with her garden hose for the dogs, who seemed quite grateful for the water after their long walk. "Maybe later... I'm thinking after she has a drink, she's probably going to want to rest after so much playing and walking. I just have to throw in some laundry and try to catch a few winks... I'm filling in for someone on the night shift tonight. Hopefully we'll hear from her owners soon."

They waved their goodbyes, and each retreated into their own side of the duplex, Patty with Barney, and Leonard with the lost dog. He retrieved his Cup O'Noodles from his briefcase, which was still sitting by the front door. The dog followed Leonard to the kitchen, and while he boiled some water for his soup, she curled up on the rug in front of the sink and went to sleep.

Since Leonard hadn't had the chance to do the crossword over breakfast as he usually did, he did it now, while he ate his Cup O'Noodles. After lunch, the dog followed Leonard into the living room, and as Leonard sat down on the sofa, the dog sat at his feet, staring up at him. "You really are a mess...um... sorry, no offense, it's just..." The dog wagged her tail. Leonard whispered, "I think you might need a bath."

Leonard had never bathed a dog before, and he was surprised at what a messy activity it was. He was also surprised at just how much dirt was swirling down the drain as he poured warm water over her fur. He lathered her up twice with his Suave Fresh Rain shampoo, and rinsed until there wasn't a trace of dirt left. He dried her fur with a fluffy bath towel. He was noticing that she wasn't such a dingy brown color, after all. Her fur was actually a lovely warm golden brown. He ended up needing another four bath towels to dry up the water from the bathroom floor, and had to change his entire outfit, which had gotten soaked through. But the dog looked and smelled so much better, and Leonard could have sworn he saw her smile.

As Leonard was bringing all the wet towels and clothes to the washer, the doorbell rang. He dropped everything in front on the washer and went to get the door. It was Patty, dressed in her colorful scrubs.

"Still no word from her owners..." she began. Just then, the dog came in from the kitchen to greet Patty.

"Oh my goodness! Did you have a bath? Did you get a nice bath, pretty girl?" The dog's tail wagged joyfully. Patty looked up at Leonard, "Wow, Leonard. I'm impressed! She looks great!"

"Didn't know what I was getting myself into. Messy business, bathing a dog."

Patty laughed. "Yes, it sure is. But you got the job done, and she looks beautiful. You know, Leonard, you seem to be a natural with dogs. Look at how she's looking at you." It was true. The dog was gazing up at Leonard adoringly.

That night, Leonard lay in bed, thinking about everything that had happened since the morning. It had been quite an eventful day, for sure. But oddly enough, in spite of its very rough start, it had turned out to be a really good day, in the end. Leonard felt at peace as he drifted off to sleep. The dog, sleeping on the rug next to his bed, sighed contentedly.

Chapter 38

October 1994

Florence was grateful to be home from the hospital, and was very much looking forward to getting to sleep in her own bed tonight. She never could rest very well in a hospital bed. After her phone call with Leonard, she had a bath, then put the kettle on for tea. She cut herself a slice of the banana bread that Evelyn had brought over, and then settled herself into Earl's recliner with her tea and bread to watch the evening news and Jeopardy.

Late that night, Florence's friend and neighbor, Evelyn, had been awakened by the sound of raccoons rummaging through her trash cans. She was such a light sleeper, but of course, Stan slept right through it. Since she was awake anyway, she figured she might as well use the bathroom. That was when she noticed the light on at Florence's house, which was very unusual. It was 2am, and Florence was most definitely not a night owl, so Evelyn worried that something might be wrong. She decided to telephone, just to be on the safe side, but there was no answer. She put on her robe, grabbed a flashlight, and woke Stan, and the two of them walked over to check on her. They knocked on the door, then rang the bell, then peered through the window.

They saw her, asleep in the recliner. Evelyn got the spare key from under the azalea bush, and the moment she crossed the threshold, she knew.

Leonard had been very sad when his father died, of course. But when he lost his mother, he was absolutely devastated. She had been the center of his world and his biggest cheerleader. She was the first person he called to share good news, and the person who lifted him up when he was feeling down. He honestly didn't know how he would go on without her.

Chapter 39

Wednesday, September 19, 2018

The phone rang at 7:25am, waking Leonard from a deep and restful sleep. It was Patty, home from the overnight shift, calling to see if he wanted to walk the dogs together. He got himself dressed and met her out front.

"Looks like you might have yourself a dog, Leonard. No one has claimed her."

"Hm." Said Leonard. "How about that."

They set off on their walk.

"I'm not sure I know how to care for a dog," said Leonard. "What if I don't know what to do?"

"First of all, you've already been taking excellent care of this little lady" Patty told him, "And second of all, I'm right next door. I've had dogs my whole life. I'm happy to help."

They walked along in silence for a bit, as Leonard considered this. "Okay, then."

When they returned to the duplex, Patty invited Leonard in for coffee, and helped him make a list of all the things he would need to buy at the pet store. She also gave him the name of her veterinarian, so he could take the dog in for a checkup and to make sure her shots were up to date, and the number for Lisa, the dog walker who took Barney out for a mid-day potty break on the days that Patty was at work.

"I tell you," Leonard said, as Patty poured them each a second cup of coffee, "I never thought I'd have a dog." He smiled at Patty. "I think I'm going to like it, though."

"I'm glad," said Patty "She really seems to have taken to you. I think she was meant to be yours."

Leonard liked the sound of that.

They sat in silence for a few moments, sipping their coffee. Leonard traced the flowers on the floral tablecloth with his finger.

"You know," he said. "My mother used to have a tablecloth like this, when I was young."

"Really?" Said Patty. "I found this one at a church rummage sale back when Todd and I first got married. I love vintage textiles. But Todd didn't like it, so I had put it away, and forgot about it. I found it again when I was moving out of my old house, packed in a box in my attic."

"A church rummage sale?" Asked Leonard.

"Yeah, down at the Episcopal church. My sisters and I love that kind of thing. Thrift shops, flea markets... it's like a treasure hunt. Never know what you'll find."

"When was it, that you bought it?" Leonard asked.

"Gosh, let me think... We were still living in our first apartment.... Probably 1994, 1995?"

Leonard smiled, looking down at the tablecloth again, then up to the ceiling, with tears in his eyes. "Well, how about that," he whispered.

Patty looked at him, quizzically. "Are you OK, there, Leonard?"

Leonard chuckled softly, then looked at Patty, still smiling. "My mother died in 1994. I donated most of her things to the Episcopal church."

Patty's eyes grew wide. "Do you think...?"

Leonard shrugged. "I'm sure other people might have had the same tablecloth, so who knows... but it's fun to think that it might be."

After they'd finished up their coffee, Leonard picked up his shopping list. "Well, I guess we'd better get going to the pet store." The dog wagged her tail as Leonard attached the leash.

"What will you name her?" Patty asked.

"Oh goodness..." said Leonard. "I don't know. I've never named anything before."

Chapter 40

October 1994

The first few days after Leonard's dear mother, God rest her soul, died, are a blur. He was grateful that his father had been such a meticulous and careful planner. Years before he had died, he had pre-purchased burial plots, and made sure their wills and final wishes were in order, so Leonard wouldn't have to worry about those details. Father James, along with Evelyn and Stan, helped Leonard with the rest of the arrangements, such as planning a reception in the church hall, for after the funeral.

The thing that Leonard remembers most about the wake and funeral was just how many people were there. He had been genuinely surprised by this. To him, Florence was just Momma, a devoted mother to him, and wife to his father. She had been the sister of his Aunt Eleanor and aunt to his cousins, Jimmy and Nancy, and dear friend to Evelyn Morris. But it seemed that there was so much more to her life, and so many people who would miss her. In addition to those he expected to see—his cousin Nancy and her family, and Stan and Evelyn Morris, and his friend Paul and his wife, and Kenneth, who drove up from Connecticut— there were also all the women from her

Book Club, the knitters from her weekly Knitting Circle, all the folks she played Bingo with on Wednesday nights, as well as her fellow congregants of the Episcopal Church, where she had attended services almost every Sunday morning her whole life. But the biggest surprise of all were the dozens of people who Leonard had never seen before... people he would soon learn had been students at the elementary school back when Florence had been the school secretary, back in the 1950s. He knew she'd worked there for many years before he was born, but he'd never really thought much about it. She had obviously made quite an impact, though, because thirty-six years later, those former students had come to pay their respects. To them, she would always be Mrs Thompson, School Secretary, who made their elementary school days brighter.

For the reception, after the funeral, the church ladies had laid out a long table with an assortment of casserole dishes, and another with desserts. Leonard knew his Momma would have loved it. Many of the mourners shared their memories with Leonard, about what a wonderful woman his mother had been. He heard stories of how she'd provided a week of meals for someone recovering from knee surgery, and how she'd collected clothes and household items for a family who'd had a house fire, and how, when she'd heard about a young family in town whose father had been laid off right before the holidays, she'd delivered a bag of toys to his home, so his children would still get a visit from Santa. She had never once mentioned any of these good deeds to Leonard, but that didn't surprise him. She'd always been the type of person to just do what needed to be done, and didn't feel the need to tell anyone about it.

When the last of the mourners had gone, Leonard began helping with the cleaning up, but Evelyn and the other church ladies insisted that they had it under control. Leonard knew from experience that there was no point in arguing with the church ladies. He thanked Father James, and Evelyn handed him some some paper plates covered in foil, patted his cheek with a wrinkled hand, and told him to go home and get some rest.

The sun was just beginning to set as he arrived home. For the first time since her passing a few days earlier, there were no preparations to attend to, no tasks to occupy his troubled mind, and no people around to distract him. As he closed and locked his front door, he was overcome with a profound and overwhelming loneliness. It began to sink in, that his mother had actually died, and he was utterly alone, in every way. He simply could not imagine how to live in the world without his mother in it. She was safety and comfort and love, and now she was gone. The grief consumed him in those quiet moments after she'd been laid to rest, leaving his body feeling like an empty husk, wispy and ungrounded. He does not even remember going to bed that night. But he does remember waking up at 6:30am the following morning, his face red and blotchy and his eyes puffy.

Not knowing what else to do, Leonard showered and shaved and dressed in chinos and a crisply ironed shirt. Then he retrieved the newspaper from the front stoop. At 6:55am, he did the crossword while he ate his Maple and Brown Sugar Quaker instant oatmeal. He made sure his breakfast dishes were washed, dried and put away before heading out to catch the 8:07 bus to Meyer & Son Manufacturing. He'd been given a week of bereavement leave, but the very idea of being left to his own devices for an entire week left him unable to breathe.

Leonard was drowning, and getting back to his regular routine was the life raft that would save him.

Some of his coworkers were surprised to see him back so soon. But Leonard just punched in, walked down to his office, and got to work, grateful to have tasks to occupy his mind, and distract himself from the deep emptiness in his chest.

Chapter 41

Thursday, September 20, 2018

Leonard looked around waiting room of the veterinarian's office. He had never been in a vet's office before. He'd assumed it would be similar to a human doctor's office waiting room— quiet and hushed, people silently reading magazines or staring at their phones— but that was not at all the case. The word "cacophony " comes to Leonard's mind. There was quite a bit of barking coming from out back, and there was a mournful meowling coming from a cat in a crate, which sat on the lap of a young woman wearing ripped jeans and a Johnny Cash tee shirt. On the bench next to the young woman, a fashionably dressed older woman sat holding a whimpering Chihuahua, who was wearing a fuzzy pink sweater and a rhinestone collar. There was a bird cage behind the receptionist desk, with an African Gray parrot, who was imitating the various animal sounds, next to a smaller cage, with a pair of singing parakeets.

When Leonard first arrived, he had been handed a clipboard by the receptionist, and was told to fill out the attached forms. He took a seat on the empty bench across from the two women, and his new dog sat politely next to his feet. He set to work filling out the intake forms. He was stumped by first on the question, at the top of the first form: *Pet's Name.* He probably should have thought of that before bringing her here. He looked around the office for inspiration. There was a basket of mums and some small pumpkins artfully arranged on a table by the door, presumably to let everyone know that it was finally autumn. Was Pumpkin a good name? No. Chrysanthemum? No, much too long. He couldn't imagine calling that across the dog park. He noticed a beam of sunlight coming in through the window. Sunny? No... sounds like Sonny. He looked out the window and saw a little boy pick a coin up from the ground and hold it up to his mother. Penny? No. Lucky? No. He reached down and scratched the dog's honey-colored fur. Honey? She gazed up at him, and wagged her tail, making a "thump thump" sound on the floor. He decided to skip that question for now, and continue with the rest of the forms.

As Leonard was finishing up with the paperwork, a woman came out of the exam room carrying a small cage containing a very fluffy rabbit, with pink eyes and floppy ears. Leonard was struck by a memory, then, of the wallpaper that had once been in his childhood bedroom. It was pale green, with yellow rabbits, and small white flowers... daisies, he thinks. That was the wallpaper his mother had chosen when she was expecting him. It remained on the walls of his room until he was nine years old, when it was finally replaced with paint the color of old blue jeans that he'd been allowed to choose himself. But he'd spent so many of his early years looking at that paper with the bunnies and daisies, that he would never, ever forget it. "Daisy" he thought. Yes, Daisy.

"Mr. Thompson?" Leonard nearly dropped the clipboard.

"Yes, right." He said, standing up, and handing the clipboard with the forms to the vet tech who'd called his name.

"Alrighty," she said, glancing at the forms, "Oh, you've forgotten one...Pet's Name..."

"Sorry... he said, "It's Daisy."

Daisy was very well-behaved as the vet performed a thorough examination, her tail wagging, making a "slap slap" sound on the metal exam table. The wagging stopped only briefly, when her first round of vaccines were administered. But all was forgiven quickly, when the vet tech offered her a treat for doing such a good job with her shots. The vet determined Daisy to be about a year old or so, a little underweight, but otherwise in good health.

"Nothing a few good meals won't fix," he said.

Chapter 42

October 1994

The Sunday after the funeral of his dear mother, God rest her soul, Leonard went to her house, at the usual time, just as he always did. As he unlocked the door and stepped inside, he half expected to see her, come walking out of the kitchen, drying her hands on her apron, same as she always did. But of course she wouldn't. She wouldn't come to greet him ever again. She couldn't, because she was gone, a fact that Leonard needed to keep reminding himself of, over and over again.

Leonard walked slowly through the rooms he knew so well, taking in every detail. He examined the curtains she'd sewn, the framed hand print, with *Happy Mother's Day* scrawled across the top that he made in kindergarten, the colorful granny square afghan she'd crocheted, draped over the sofa and the collection of Hummel figurines and other knickknacks on the shelves. He stopped to look at the framed photos on the hallway wall. There was a picture of his parents on their wedding day, pictures of Leonard and his parents together, and pictures of the three of them, and some with the other relatives, taken on family vacations and holidays. Leonard looked closely at a photo taken at Grandma Alice's house, on Christmas Day in 1967, when he was eight years old. It's a picture of the whole family: Leonard and his parents, Grandma Alice, Aunt Eleanor, Uncle James, and Leonard's cousins, Jimmy and Nancy. It turned out to be the last Christmas they spent with Jimmy, and the last photo they had of him. That winter, he was deployed to Vietnam, and was killed in combat. His death had been a devastating blow to the family; a disruption to the natural order of things. Parents and grandparents are not supposed to outlive their children and grandchildren. Now, twenty-seven years later, it was only Leonard and Nancy who were left. She married a dentist in 1969, and is now the mother of two grown daughters.

On the opposite wall of the hallway, there were thirteen frames of Leonard, one for each grade, from Kindergarten to Grade 12. Leonard smiled, and shook his head. He hated those photos. Especially the ones from sixth to tenth grade. Those were by far his most awkward years, when he'd had braces on his teeth to go along with his thick glasses, and spots of hormonal acne popping up on his face. They didn't airbrush school photos back in those days, so every little blemish was preserved for posterity.

He continued on to the bathroom, where her toothbrush still sat in the glass, the towel still hung on the hook. On the tank of the toilet stood the doll with a spare roll of toilet paper under her crocheted dress. He stopped at the doorway to the bedroom. Her bed was perfectly made, the pillows artfully arranged. There was a book on the nightstand, with a bookmark in it. Leonard went over, and picked it up. "*Chicken Soup for the Soul...* of course..." he whispered, smiling to himself.

Back in the kitchen, he made himself a grilled cheese sandwich and heated up a can of tomato soup. He ate his lunch alone at the kitchen table. Then, he took out the air conditioner and mowed the lawn. Over the next few months, Leonard returned to the house every Sunday afternoon, and began slowly boxing up the contents of his parents' lives. Some things, of sentimental value, such as the family photo albums, his father's collection of old books, the family bible, and the granny square afghan were brought back to the condo. He was thinking his cousin Nancy might like to have Grandma Alice's silver tea set. Her knitting basket, filled with balls of yarn and needles, and a half-completed sweater, would be dropped off to the Knitting Circle Ladies. But the rest of his parents' things would be donated. Father James would help distribute the clothing, housewares and furnishings to needy families in the community, and the rest would go to the church's annual rummage sale.

Once the house was empty, Leonard scrubbed it from top to bottom, and called a Realtor. It was purchased by a young couple, newly married and expecting a baby soon. Leonard knew that his dear mother, God rest her soul, would be so pleased to know that another couple was going to raise their child in this house, as she and his father had.

It took Leonard a very long time to get used to not going to his parents house. He knew he'd never stop missing them, but he eventually settled into a new routine, and carried on the best he could.

Chapter 43

Friday, September 21, 2018

Leonard sat at the kitchen table, and did the crossword puzzle while he ate his Maple and Brown Sugar Quaker Instant Oatmeal. Daisy ate her kibble from her shiny new bowl, which was set up in the corner of the kitchen, on a little place mat printed with little dog bones.

After breakfast, he made sure the dishes were washed, dried and put away, because "A tidy home is a happy home" as his dear mother, God rest her soul, used to say. When he finished, he noticed Daisy was sitting patiently in front of the door.

"Oh." Leonard said, "Do you want to go out?" Daisy wagged her tail, and gave a short bark in reply. "OK then. Let's go to the Dog Park." He put on his shoes and jacket, and retrieved Daisy's new pink leash from the hook by the front door. He clipped the leash to her new pink collar, and they headed out together.

The morning air was crisp, but the sun was already shining up in the clear blue sky. Leonard looked around as they walked, noticing that the leaves were starting to change, smudges of yellow and orange appearing among the green. He heard loud chirping coming from a large shrub in someone's front yard, and noticed that there were dozens of the same type of birds in there. Leonard imagined it was perhaps some sort of avian rest stop, on their migratory journey. He noticed small children with little backpacks walking with their mothers, and a man coming out of the cafe with a to-go cup, holding the door for the older woman who was on her way in. He noticed squirrels picking up acorns from under the big oak tree by the library. It occurred to Leonard that it had been quite some time since he'd really truly *noticed* things. His neighborhood, his community, the natural world around him. How on earth had he been missing all of this?

At the dog park, Daisy made friends with a black lab puppy named Cleo, and they chased each other around happily. The puppy's owner, a younger man dressed in jeans and a college sweatshirt, commented on what a nice dog Daisy was, which made Leonard feel proud. Leonard pointed to the young man's sweatshirt.

"Are you a student there?" He asked.

"Yes, just starting my senior year. Computer Science." The young man replied.

Leonard nodded. "I graduated from there in 1980. Accounting."

The young man smiled broadly, and extended a hand to Leonard. "Wow, a fellow Jackrabbit!"

Leonard chuckled, and shook the young man's hand. "Well, I was there before the Jackrabbit..."

"Right, the old mascot..." the young man said with a grimace. The college had retired its former mascot, an offensive racial stereotype, about ten years earlier.

"I prefer the Jackrabbit." Leonard said with a wink. He pointed over to the dogs. "Looks like Cleo's tired from running around." She was lying in the grass, and Daisy was sitting beside her.

"Aw... I better get her home. It was nice to meet you...I'm Noah, by the way."

"I'm Leonard. It was nice meeting you and Cleo, Noah."

When they returned home an hour later, there was a package sitting on the door mat. "My, that was quick!" Leonard thought to himself as he picked up the package and unlocked the door. After filling Daisy's shiny new water bowl, he opened the package. It was the new alarm clock he had ordered online. He had tried to find one that looked like the one his mother had given him all those years ago; an analog alarm clock, with two little bells on top. This one wasn't exactly the same, but it was close enough. Daisy followed him to the bedroom, where he set the clock to the correct time, set up the alarm for 6:30am, then placed the clock on the nightstand by the lamp, right where the old one had been. He sat on the edge of the bed, holding the old clock. He thought back to the day of his college graduation, when his mother had given it to him. He thought about how proud his parents had been, and how his mother had always been so steadfast in her love and support of him. The clock was no longer functional, but he couldn't part with it. He wrapped it up carefully in the packaging from the new clock, and put the box up on the top shelf of his closet. When he finished, Daisy was lying in her fluffy new dog bed next to Leonard's bed. He crouched down next to her and stroked her honey-colored fur.

"I have to go run an errand." He whispered to her. "You have yourself a good rest, and I'll be back soon."

Chapter 44

December 23, 2014

As Leonard walked home from the bus stop, he looked up at the snowflakes falling in the glow of the streetlights. It really was quite lovely. He always enjoyed the first snow of the season. There was just something a little bit magical about it. When he reached the house, he saw Patty sitting on her side of the stoop, putting four small snow boots on Barney's paws. The boots matched the red quilted jacket he was wearing. Patty was wearing a big red Santa Hat, and earrings that looked like Christmas tree ornaments.

"Leonard!" Patty exclaimed. "Looks like we're going to have a White Christmas this year!"

"Looks that way." He said. "You and Barney are looking festive."

"Thanks! I'm working on Christmas Eve and Christmas, so we're heading over to my sister Bonnie's house tonight instead. We're doing a "Secret Santa" gift swap."

"That sounds nice. Do you always work Christmas?"

"Usually. I always offer to take shifts for nurses who have little ones at home, so they can enjoy the whole Santa thing with them. I figure, since I don't have kids..." She shrugged.

Leonard nodded. "Well, that's very nice of you."

Patty waved off the compliment. "Nah, it's not a big deal. I don't mind doing it. How about you? Do you have family nearby?

"I do. Some... I was an only child, but I do have a cousin who's about an hour away. I'll be having dinner with them on Christmas."

"Well that's nice. Are you close?"

He smiled uncomfortably. "Um, not really? She was a teenager when I was born, so we didn't grow up together or anything like that. Our mothers were sisters, so when I was a child, our families got together often. We even used to go on vacations together. But, after our parents' died, we didn't see each other very much. Usually just Thanksgiving and sometimes Christmas."

"Oh, that's too bad," Patty said, sympathetically.

"It's OK. We don't have much in common aside from our ancestors. But it is nice to reminisce a couple of times a year with someone who knew my parents. I'm grateful for that." Said Leonard.

"That is important."

Leonard nodded.

"Well, Leonard, I hope you have a wonderful Christmas." Patty finished lacing up Barney's last boot. "We need to get going... Bonnie hates it when I'm late. But first.... Stay right there! I have something for you! I was hoping I'd catch you before tomorrow."

She handed the end of Barney's leash to Leonard over the railing between their stoops, and dashed inside, returning seconds later with a cellophane-wrapped plate of sugar cookies in assorted Christmas shapes, decorated with colorful, sparkling sugar. She handed the plate to Leonard, trading the cookies for Barney's leash. "Merry Christmas!"

"For me?" Leonard almost whispered. No one had baked him Christmas cookies since his dear mother, God rest her soul, had passed away.

"Of course for you! You like cookies, don't you?"

"Yes... yes, thank you. I...um..." He nodded. "Merry Christmas."

"Merry Christmas, Leonard." Said Patty, waving as she headed down the steps with Barney.

Chapter 45

Saturday, September 22, 2018

Leonard woke up at 6:30am, and got himself dressed and ready for the day. He and Daisy were meeting Patty and Barney for a walk before breakfast.

"Good Morning!" Called Patty when she saw them. Leonard noticed that she was dressed in jeans and a cotton sweater instead of her scrubs.

"Morning." Said Leonard, as the dogs sniffed each other, tails wagging. "Day off for you, today?"

"Yes!" Patty replied, as they set off for the dog park. "I'm planning to go over to the garden center later, and get some mums. A little treat for myself."

"That's nice." Said Leonard. "Nursing is a very hard job, I would imagine... you certainly deserve a treat on your day off."

Patty smiled. "Well, thank you. It is hard, sometimes. Working in the Emergency Department is not for the faint of heart. But for some reason, I love it."

"I think the reason is that nurses are very special people. I could never do what you do. It sounds terrifying to me." Leonard said.

"Oh, please.. we're not special. We're just getting through the day like everyone else."

Leonard rolled his eyes. "Patty, 'everyone else' isn't saving lives as a regular part of their work day. Don't downplay what you do. You should be proud of your work."

Patty nodded. "Well, OK. Thank you. I am proud, I suppose. I'm better at being a nurse than I am at taking a compliment. What about you? Are you proud of your work?"

They walked in silence for a moment, as Leonard thought about this. "I think I used to be. But, I'm realizing lately that my job isn't really that important. I mean, I'm most definitely not saving any lives."

"But Leonard," Patty said. "Without you, people wouldn't get their paychecks! That's important."

"Without me, someone else would do it. Everyone would still get paid." He shrugged. "Speaking of work, I guess I'm going back on Monday. Week went by fast." said Leonard.

"Yes... Did you reach Lisa?"

"I did. She's going to take both Daisy and Barney out at 1pm."

"I think you'll be happy with her. Barney just loves her... I'm sure Daisy will, too."

"Oh... by the way..." Leonard said. "I have something to show you." They stopped walking while he reached into his his back pocket. He pulled out an iPhone and held it up.

"Leonard! You got a cell phone!" Patty laughed and hugged him.

Leonard blushed. "Yeah. I'm still not quite sure what to do with it. The guy at the phone store showed me some things, but it's kind of a lot..."

"You'll figure it out. It's easier than you think. Wow, I'm really proud of you."

When they got back home, Leonard ate his oatmeal and did the crossword, while Daisy ate her kibble, then Leonard cleaned up the house, did his laundry and ironed all of his shirts for the week. After he had his peanut butter and jelly sandwich for lunch, he headed out, list in hand, to run his errands.

Patty was outside, planting some gold and burgundy mums in her window box. Leonard also noticed she had a new wreath on the door, with red, orange and yellow leaves, acorns, and a big, burlap bow. As Leonard made his way down the steps with his shopping list, she made a dramatic gesture of looking at her watch and winked at Leonard.

Later, Leonard stood in the cereal aisle at the grocery store, scanning the boxes of Quaker Instant Oatmeal, in search of the Maple and Brown Sugar flavor. He saw Apple Cinnamon, Raisins and Spice, Peaches and Cream, Original, and a variety pack, but no Maple and Brown Sugar.

Leonard sighed.

Then, he reached for the Variety Pack, and dropped it into his shopping cart.

Chapter 46

August 2005

As Leonard was typing out a memo regarding the new time card system, he noticed the time on the corner of his computer screen: 11:59am. He closed his word processing program and opened his bottom left desk drawer to retrieve his Cup O'Noodles. Then, he headed down the hallway to the break room, closing his office door behind him on his way out.

As he came into the break room, he first saw Dot, the HR manager, Margaret Olson, who worked in Accounts Receivable, and Dolores, Mr. Meyer's secretary, who yelled "SURPRISE!" as they gestured to a cake, in a way that reminded Leonard of TV game show hostesses revealing a grand prize. The cake had "Congratulations Leonard - 25 years! - " written in orange icing. Several other employees were there, as well, and they clapped as Leonard blushed, and looked down at his shoes. The biggest surprise by far was that Mr. Meyer was there, too. It occurred to Leonard that he had never seen Mr. Meyer in the break room, ever. Certainly not since he took over as president of Meyer & Son when his father retired five years ago. But not before then, either. It was clear that the only reason he was there now was because of Dolores. She had been the senior Mr Meyer's secretary for almost eight years before she became the younger Mr Meyer's secretary. She was the only person at Meyer & Son who had any sway over the younger Mr. Meyer, and she had insisted that he continue his father's tradition of personally congratulating employee milestones.

"Wow," said Leonard, still blushing. "Wow! I don't know what to say... Thank you."

"Margaret made the cake," said Dot. "And..." she looked to Mr. Meyer, who was staring down at his Blackberry.

Dolores elbowed him in the ribs. Mr. Meyer looked up, oblivious, and Dolores pointed to the table.

"Oh! Right." He said, picking up a wood plaque from the table, and handing it to Leonard. "Congratulations, Leonard. Twenty-five years! Hey! You've been working here ten years longer than me!" Leonard smiled awkwardly as Mr. Meyer gave him a half-hearted pat on the back, and said, "Keep up the good work."

And with that, Mr. Meyer headed toward the door, calling, "Hey Dolores, save me a piece of cake!" as he headed back down the hall.

"That man is an ass." Said Dot, shaking her head. Dolores, Margaret, and a few of the other employees nodded in agreement.

Although it had been five years since the first Mr. Meyer retired, many of the older employees still found it hard to believe that pain-in-the-ass, Chip Meyer, was now in charge of the company. It was generally believed by most of the employees that Dolores was the only reason he hadn't run it into the ground yet.

Leonard looked down at the plaque in his hands. It was made

of dark wood, with a brass plate attached to the front, which said:

Meyer & Son Manufacturing
in recognition of
25 Years of Service
presented to
Leonard J. Thompson

"Cut the cake, Leonard!" Margaret said, handing him a knife and a stack of paper plates. "It's carrot cake."

Leonard set the plaque down on the table, and took the knife and plates. "Carrot cake is my favorite."

"I know!" Margaret said, "you mentioned that when I brought in carrot cake for Dot's birthday."

He paused for a moment, holding the knife above the cake. He was touched that she had noticed, and remembered. "That is so thoughtful of you... "

Margaret interrupted him with a wave of her hand.

"Oh, stop it. With all hard work you do, and the nonsense you put up with around here, you deserve to have a cake you like."

Leonard blushed, and murmured a thank you. He found it very awkward to accept a compliment.

After Leonard had finished eating his Cup O'Noodles and his piece of carrot cake, he headed back to his office with his new plaque. Although he wasn't the type to enjoy being the center of attention, he did think that it was very kind of his coworkers to recognize him. Hanging on the wall behind his desk, there were three other plaques, for ten years, fifteen years and twenty years of service. He looked up at the plaques on the wall, and then stared down at the plaque in his hands. He was practically a kid, still living with his parents, when he started here. And now, he was nearly a half-century old, and he was still here. Where on Earth had the time gone?

Chapter 47

Sunday, September 23, 2018

Leonard woke up at precisely 6:30am. After he showered, shaved, and dressed in chinos and a crisply ironed shirt, he took Daisy out for a walk to do her business. When they returned, he retrieved the newspaper from the front stoop. At 7:15am, he filled Daisy's bowl with kibble, then prepared his soft boiled egg and toast, which he ate while doing the Sunday crossword. After he cleaned up from breakfast, Daisy was sleeping on the kitchen rug, so Leonard fixed himself a second cup of coffee, and sat back down at the kitchen table to read the Sunday paper, as usual.

As he turned the page to the Local News section, a photo caught his eye. The photo was a mugshot, of a balding man whose remaining hair was wispy and disheveled, a bewildered expression on his face. Leonard thought that the person in the photo looked familiar, somehow... though, to his knowledge, he did not personally know any criminals. The caption under the photo read: *Officer John Allen Arrested, held without bail.*

"Oh my... " he said to himself. "That's Johnny Allen!"

While Leonard was quite surprised to see that Johnny had

become a police officer in the next town over, he was not at all surprised to see that Johnny had engaged in illegal activity. He had always known that guy to be bad news. He read the accompanying article:

"Police Officer Arrested"

"A Brookshire police officer was arrested on Saturday, after numerous reports from motorists who claimed that they'd been assaulted and robbed during traffic stops within the town. An investigation ensued, spurred by a tip from the estranged wife of the accused, who had recently taken out a restraining order against him. The arrest was made during a sting operation in which the accused officer, John Leonard Allen,"

Leonard stopped reading, and put down the paper. John *Leonard* Allen? Johnny Allen's middle name is Leonard?? Leonard Thompson is not one to use foul language, generally speaking, but the phrase that came to mind in that particular moment was: "What the actual fuck."

After a moment, Leonard picked the paper up and began reading again.

"... during a sting operation in which the accused officer, John Leonard Allen, assaulted an undercover State Police officer. A search of Allen's apartment was conducted, and large stashes of cash, jewelry, and prescription drugs were recovered, all of which had previously been reported stolen by the motorists who had reported being targeted by Allen."

Leonard stared at the mugshot, taking in the adult version of his childhood tormentor. The boy who had mercilessly bullied Leonard, without remorse, for twelve long years, had lived in his memory as confident, strong and tough... a threatening presence who left Leonard always looking over his shoulder.

But the man in this photo was none of those things. He just looked pathetic.

That afternoon, he and Daisy went on a long afternoon walk. Leonard thought about how he'd be going back to work at Meyer & Son the next day, and it occurred to him that he really didn't want to. Just six days ago he'd been filled dread at the notion of *not* going to Meyer & Son, and now, for the first time in thirty-seven years, Leonard was thinking that it might be time for a change in his employment situation.

For many years, Leonard genuinely enjoyed his job. He had learned a lot in his early years of employment there, and had felt quite a sense of accomplishment when the first Mr Meyer put him in charge of Payroll for the whole company. It's a position which involves handling a variety of responsibilities, and requires meticulous attention to detail, so Leonard has always found it to be satisfying work. The first Mr Meyer was the type of boss who knew the names of all his employees, and treated everyone, from the department supervisors to the lady who emptied the trash cans and cleaned the offices, with kindness and respect. The first Mr Meyer worked hard, and he expected the same from his employees, but he was also fair and kind; all qualities that Leonard has always found admirable. Chip Meyer, on the other hand, while admittedly less of a fuck up than he once was, is still a pain-in-the-ass, and in the seventeen years since he's been in charge, Leonard has found that the experience of working at Meyer & Son has gone downhill considerably.

Chapter 48

Sunday, September 23, 2018

When Leonard and Daisy returned from their Sunday walk, Patty and her niece, Sophie, were sitting on the stoop with Barney. Once a month or so, Patty and Sophie had a sleepover at Patty's. Leonard noticed that Patty and Barney had several sparkly clips adorning their hair and fur, and Patty and Sophie both had each of their fingernails painted different colors.

"Leonard!" Said Patty as he and Daisy approached the duplex.

Sophie's face lit up when she saw Daisy.

"That's Daisy, Leonard's new dog!" Patty told her. "Isn't she pretty?"

Barney got up greet Daisy. "Aw, they're friends!" Said Sophie.

Daisy's tail wagged enthusiastically as Patty and Sophie fussed over her, giving her scritches and cooing about what a good girl she is.

When Patty's sister, Kelly, pulled up in front of the house, Sophie jumped up. "Mom!" She called, "Leonard got a dog! Her name is Daisy and she's friends with Barney!"

Sophie climbed into the backseat of the car, and Patty handed her a unicorn backpack. Patty and Leonard waved to Kelly and

Sophie as they drove off.

"I tell you," said Patty, "I love that sweet child with my whole heart, but, wow, it takes a lot of energy, keeping up with a ten-year-old!!" She sat down on the stoop next to Daisy, and asked her, "Did you have fun joining Leonard on his Sunday walk?"

"I think she did." Said Leonard with a smile. "And I enjoyed her company."

Patty squinted at Leonard, then. "Okay, so I've always wanted to ask... what is the deal with your Sunday walks? Since I've lived here, no matter the weather, every Sunday, you head out for a walk at one o'clock, and come back around four. Three hours is a very long walk. Where do you go?"

Leonard was quiet for a moment, then cleared his throat. "I go to visit my parents." He said.

Patty looked very confused, her brow furrowed. "But..."

Leonard laughed. "I go to Evergreen Cemetery." Patty looked relieved. "When they were still alive, I used to go to their house every Sunday afternoon, to visit. And after they died, well... I missed those visits. I still do. I started going to the cemetery after I sold their house, because I just didn't know what else to do on Sundays. But then I started to enjoy it. Is a nice walk, and... I don't know. I guess I just like that I have a place to go, to talk to them." He shrugged.

"That's lovely, Leonard. My mom is also buried at Evergreen."

"Well, if you and Barney ever want to join us, you're welcome to." Leonard told her.

Patty smiled. "I would like that. Thank you. But right now," she said, standing up, "I need some coffee... care to join me?"

"I'd love to, but I have something to take care of." said Leonard.

"Sounds mysterious..." said Patty.

Leonard smiled. "Not so mysterious. I just need to write a letter of resignation."

Patty gasped. "Whaaat?!?" She exclaimed, eyes wide.

"Yeah. I'm a little surprised, too. It's just... well, I realized it's time. Having this week off made me realize that I haven't actually enjoyed working there in a very a long time. I just stayed because I didn't really know what else to do." Said Leonard. Patty stared at him, speechless. "I know..." he said. "It's unexpected."

"Leonard, I am a woman who has seen some shit. It is very hard to shock me. But let me tell you... I. Am. Shocked. Did not see this coming!" Said Patty, shaking her head.

"Me neither... " said Leonard with a little chuckle.

"So what's next, Leonard? What's your plan?"

Leonard shrugged. "Well, I'm 60 years old. I've been at Meyer & Son since I was twenty-two. Almost 38 years. I really can't imagine working anywhere else, but I also can't imagine staying there anymore. I have a 401K, and plenty of savings. I figured I'd take early retirement, spend some time here with Daisy, and figure it out from there."

Patty shook her head in amazement. "Well, I never thought I'd see the day. Not in a million years. Leonard Thompson, embracing change."

Leonard was somewhat surprised by how easy it was to compose his resignation letter, considering he'd never written one before. After he finished typing it up, he went to the kitchen to feed Daisy and heat up his can of Campbell's chicken noodle soup. After dinner, he washed, dried and put away the dishes, because, as his dear mother, God rest her soul, used to say, "A tidy home is a happy home." Then he went back to the computer to proofread his letter. Once he was satisfied with it, he printed it out, tucked it into an envelope, and put it in his briefcase. He'll give it to Mr. Meyer first thing tomorrow morning. With that matter settled, he picked up his iPhone and sent Patty a text.

Hello Patty,

I'm going to take Daisy out for her evening walk in a few minutes.

Would you and Barney like to join us?

Leonard

Almost as soon as he set the phone back down on the desk, it buzzed.

OMG Leonard UR texting!!! Yes to walk... be right out.

Epilogue

2023

Leonard J. Thompson wakes up every morning at precisely 6:30am. He showers, shaves, and dresses in chinos and a crisply ironed shirt, and puts on the engraved watch he received as a gift when he retired from Meyer & Son Manufacturing. Then, he takes his dog, Daisy, out for her morning walk. When they return, he retrieves the newspaper from the front stoop. At 7:30am, he feeds Daisy, then he does the crossword puzzle while he eats his Quaker Instant Oatmeal. Sometimes he has the Cinnamon Spice flavor, or the Peaches and Cream. Sometimes he has Strawberry or Raisins and Spice. Sometimes he has the Maple and Brown Sugar flavor. His dear mother, God rest her soul, always said, "A tidy home is a happy home," so he always makes sure his breakfast dishes are washed, dried and put away before he heads out the door.

On Monday mornings, he volunteers at the library.

On Tuesday mornings, he goes to his pottery class, down at the Senior Center.

On Wednesday mornings, he and Patty volunteer at the local animal shelter.

On Thursday mornings, he swims at the YMCA.

On Friday mornings, he and Daisy, now a Certified Therapy Dog, visit the VA hospital.

In the afternoons, Leonard and Daisy walk down to the dog park. On the days when Patty isn't working at the hospital, she and her puppy, Charlie, join them. While they watch the dogs play, Patty and Leonard sit on the carved wooden bench that he donated to the dog park last year, as a surprise for Patty. There is a brass plaque on the back of the bench that says:

In Memory of

Barney

2009-2022

In the years since his retirement, Leonard has been learning how to cook, so he doesn't eat nearly as much Campbell's soup as he used to. He has Patty to thank for this. She has taught him to make quite a few things, like lasagna, tofu stir fry, stuffed peppers, and three-bean chili. They usually cook dinner together at least once a week.

In the evenings, Leonard still enjoys settling in with a good book, with Daisy curled up by his side. And of course, he is always in bed by 9:00pm, because, as his dear mother, God rest her soul, always said, "Early to bed, early to rise, makes a man healthy, wealthy and wise."

In October, Patty turned sixty. Her sisters, Bonnie and Kelly, and her best friend, Leonard, rented the VFW hall and threw a huge surprise party for her. Her niece, Sophie, baked a gorgeous cake, decorated with pretty sugar flowers. Her nephew Max, and his fiancée Elizabeth, decorated the hall with streamers and a huge "Happy Birthday" banner. Patty's nephew Caleb was the DJ, and his husband, Jake, who works for a catering company, set up an impressive buffet. Patty's friends from the hospital, the dog park, and the animal shelter were all there, too. Before they cut the birthday cake, Caleb lifted Max and Elizabeth's toddler, Patricia, up onto his shoulder, and held the microphone as she sang "Happy Birthday" to her great aunt Patty. It was, as you might expect, completely adorable. Although Leonard has never much cared for parties, he had a wonderful time at this one.

In December, Leonard and Patty decided to ring in the New Year together, with the dogs. They all sat on Patty's sofa, in her colorful living room, Leonard at one end, Patty at the other, with Daisy and Charlie between them. Leonard was wearing a cardboard top hat with "2024" written in glitter across it. Patty was wearing a glittery cardboard tiara that said, "Happy New Year" on it. They each held a glass of champagne, and as the ball dropped on the TV screen, they shouted, "Happy New Year!" and blew their party blowers. Then, they clinked their glasses together over the dogs' heads.

"To best friends," said Patty.

"To best friends, and new adventures," said Leonard.

The End

About the Author

Jenney Cheever never really knew how to answer the question, "What do you want to be when you grow up?" But it worked out fine, as her uncertain career aspirations have led to many interesting adventures, such as teaching preschool, writing and performing sketch comedy, making art, teaching and performing with a children's theater company, writing articles for an online publication, beekeeping, professional home organizing, running a small homestead farm, and going back to college in her 50's. Her favorite adventure of all has been raising her three amazing children. Jenney now lives in beautiful Western Massachusetts, where she can often be found either tending her garden, or tackling her latest DIY project. *A Creature of Habit* is her first book.

You can connect with me on:

🔗 https://linktr.ee/JenneyCheever